BLOOD BONES

Garrett Boatman

BLOODY BONES

BLOODY BONES

Garrett Boatman

Cemetery Dance Publications
Baltimore
2025

Cemetery Dance Publications
132B Industry Lane, Unit #7
Forest Hill, MD 21050
www.cemeterydance.com

Trade Paperback Edition
ISBN: 978-1-964780-38-2

Cover Artwork © 2025 by Lynne Hansen
Interior/Ebook Design, Cover Layout/Typography © 2025 by Steven Pajak

For my grandmother
Lima Francis McFarland
who taught me to love scary stories

ONE

1924

She looked up at the man who led her through the pine woods. He was very tall against the twilight, his jaw as square as his broad shoulders. It seemed to her he might be handsome, if only he smiled.

"Here, child," the man said in his curious speech. The man pushed aside a screen of pine branches and herded her onto a deer path that led through a tangle of huge ferns. She could hear the creek now, gurgling up ahead. The stars were coming out between the pines.

The man had said he was a preacher. He was dressed all in black except for a white shirt. Even his shiny, sharp-creased tie was black. And like Reverend Walker, the preacher at the Mt. Zion Baptist Church, which she and her mama attended, the man didn't smile. And like Reverend Walker, midway through the service, sweaty-faced in the hot one-room church, the man's face shone.

Mama hurt!

She felt close to tears. How was Mama hurt? How had it happened? Was Mama going to die?

She was too shy to ask, and the man had hardly spoken since stopping her on the road on her way home from the grocery store and telling her that her mother was hurt.

"Not much farther." He released her hand. "There."

She squinted into the gathering gloom, seeing only pines and darkness.

"Where?"

Behind her, she heard the rustle of leaves as he picked up something from the ground. She turned.

The branch struck the left side of her mouth with a loud *crack,* knocking out two teeth and spraying bark and blood. Her mama's five-pound bag of flour exploded when it hit the ground, whitewashing nearby ferns.

Barely conscious, she was only dimly aware of her panties being ripped off, of his rough hands closing around her throat, of the new explosion of pain that tore through her body.

TWO

1956

"I Bloody Bones, an' I on the porch." Pa's low voice, dramatically spooky, sent shivers crawling like spiders up the boy's spine. "Can't you hear the creak of that loose board your pa been meanin' to fix?"

The boy listened. Besides his heart's excited beating, he heard the sough of the breeze under the eaves and the soft brushing of pine needles against the roof shingles, like the fingers of a skeleton scratching to get in.

"Don't you hear it?"

The boy's heart beat faster and, indeed, he heard a creak that could have been the house settling or might very well have been a porch board.

"Yes, sir."

"I Bloody Bones, an' I comin' to get you." Pa's gravelly whisper made the boy think of ghosts.

"I Bloody Bones, an' I in the house," Pa continued. "Listen. Can't you hear my footsteps outside your curtain?"

The boy listened. He heard the soft *creak-creak* of Mama's chair rocking out there on the other side of the curtain that separated his bed from the main part of the cabin. And he heard another sound—*clomp-clomp-clomp*.

He shivered again, even though he knew Pa was making the sounds with his heavy work boots on the pine boards.

"I Bloody Bones, an' I comin' to get you."

The boy shuddered at what came next. Though he had heard the story often, he shivered in delicious anticipation.

"I Bloody Bones, an' I in your room."

The boy hunkered down in his bed so that only his eyes and hands showed above the edge of the sheet. All of a sudden, the beating of his heart was louder. It wasn't so bad when Bloody Bones was "in the yard" or "on the porch" or "outside your curtain"—so long as he was "out there," you were still safe; but once he was "in your room," it was all over.

"I Bloody Bones, and I standin' by your bed. Can't you see the blood drippin' from my bones?"

The boy squeezed his eyes shut to keep out the frightening vision, but the skeleton, not to be stopped by eyelids, grinned at him, blood dripping from the pale skull, red eyes glowing like a jack-o'-lantern's. Smiling, the boy tensed for the end.

"I Bloody Bones, and—I GOTCHA!"

And then the man was tickling him and he was laughing, and the laughter was like a rubber band unwinding, releasing the tension that had built up during the tale.

And his pa laughed with him. And when his mother called in to them to settle down because it was late and time for little boys to rest and Pa tucked him in and kissed him good night, sleep wasn't long in coming.

THREE

The noise of the boys' running and shouting rose with the heat into the sun-dappled trees. Ahead, Mauser's barking was getting louder, which told Steven the big Doberman had stopped and they were catching up.

Steven's close-cropped, copper-colored hair flashed in the sun and the collar of his blue-and-white striped shirt flapped as he hung back with Jimmy and Whitey, the three of them jogging along behind Billy Bob, the Sheriff's son and Mauser's owner. Only Skeeter and Lance, who had both disappeared from sight, were foolhardy enough to try to reach Mauser before Billy Bob. Steven could picture them, Lance keeping behind Skeeter, in case Mauser turned. Skeeter with a big yahoo grin on his thin face, kicking dust, too dumb to be afraid.

"Probably treed a possum!" Billy Bob huffed over his shoulder. His heavy legs pounded the earth; a long V of sweat darkened the back of his tee shirt.

His neck wasn't wider than his head like the Sheriff's, nor as red, but it was thick and sunburnt, and his hair was cut Marine style same as his pa's. In spite of being called "fatso or "that fat so and so" (behind his back, of course), there was enough muscle pumping under the fat to make Billy Bob Wilcox the most feared and respected bully in the seventh grade at the Fox School.

Crashing through a thicket, they emerged into a weedy clearing baking under the hot Georgia sun, and there was Mauser, snarling and barking and practically foaming at the mouth as he stood on his hind legs and clawed bark from the oak. Something, indeed, had been treed by the Doberman. Coming up behind Skeeter and Lance, Steven saw it.

"There it is!" shouted Whitey, who could almost pass for an albino.

Peering down at them from a high branch, the possum blinked and disappeared.

"Good boy, Mauser! Get 'im!" Billy Bob roared, and Mauser went at the tree with renewed frenzy. Billy Bob's tee shirt had rode up on his sweaty belly. He stood with his hands on his wide hips, chest heaving as he caught his breath, perspiration dripping from his double chin.

The possum showed its head again and Skeeter whooped and fetched up a stone and sent it whizzing at the furry head. He missed and let out a disgusted, "Yah!"

Whitey, overcome with excitement, giggled, and Skeeter turned on him, beady brown eyes narrowing, a scowl darkening his long, freckled face.

"You laughin' at me, Boy?" Skeeter—who was tall, gangling, and the second-worst bully in the seventh grade after Billy Bob—had big feet and big hands and loved to punch younger kids as much as he enjoyed yanking the legs off frogs or putting the eyes out of fish before tossing them back into the water. His ratty hair clung to his forehead. His freckles bunched menacingly on his cheeks.

"N-no!" Whitey yelped, his pink skin turning two shades darker, becoming clearly visible through his white hair.

Skeeter smiled, showing crooked, green teeth; but his face remained dark and his big hands curled into fists.

"Yeah, you did too!" he corrected. "I don't like nobody laughin' at me!"

Mauser continued his barking, seemingly without stopping to breathe.

Billy Bob and Lance looked amused, Billy's small blue eyes narrowing, Lance's brown eyes twinkling craftily.

Whitey dropped his gaze.

"Leave him alone, *Francis*," Jimmy said, stepping between Skeeter and Whitey. Steven thought Jimmy looked a lot like his dad right now with that easy smile on his lips. Course, he didn't have long sideburns and he didn't smoke Lucky Strikes, but he had the same thin triangular face and wide green eyes and he wore the sleeves of his white tee shirt rolled up like his truck-driving dad.

Francis "Skeeter" Mulligan, who hated being called by his real name as much as he loved running between the swings on the playground and tossing sand into girls' faces as they swooped down, pigtails flying, mouths open, turning their laughter into shouts of distress and anger, glared at the wiry, deeply tanned, black-haired boy. Jimmy was grinning, but his fists were clenched, and all Skeeter did was say, "You gonna make me?"

"Naw," Jimmy Earl Dobbins drawled like he was bored. "I wouldn't waste my spit."

Skeeter's face turned a shade darker and he glanced at Lance for support, but Lance was conveniently observing the treed possum. Steven, who watched the exchange, knew that, although Lance liked to see Billy Bob or Skeeter whack the daylights out of smaller kids, he was afraid of getting his pretty face messed up.

Then Lance was pointing. "Hey! Looky there!" And they all looked; even Mauser ceased his racket to see why they'd shushed.

In a patch of blue beyond the oak hung a small white diamond shape bobbing and dancing in the breeze, tiny with distance and with a fluttering red and yellow ribbon hanging below.

"Somebody flyin' a kite," Billy Bob said unnecessarily.

"Way on up there, ain't it?" Whitey said, shading his eyes with his hand

"Flour and newspaper kite," Steven commented.

"Come on!" Billy Bob yelled and took off running with Mauser loping at his side.

MRS. LAVONNE LITTLE WAS OUT BACK WITH HER WASH basket taking the clothes off the line. Bean vines coiled up strings attached to her clothesline poles. Nearby was her vegetable garden followed by a stretch of lawn running down to the barbwire fence.

Of course, the barbwire fence had a hole in it, as fences generally do when there's a boy around who wants to get to what's on the other side. In this case, what was on the other side was one of Mr. Grierson's fields and, beyond that, the woods bordering the swamp and a big wide-open meadow just inside the woods.

Mrs. Little couldn't see the meadow through the screen of trees, but she could see Lamar's kite soaring and dipping way up in the blue. Lamar and his pa had made the kite yesterday evening before Reginald put the boy to bed and told him a story.

As she plucked a row of socks from the line, dropping the clothes pins into her apron pocket each time she had a fistful, Lavonne reflected how happy Reginald was to be working again. He wasn't as spry as he used to be. He'd been laid up with a sprained back for ten days last month, then couldn't find work for two weeks. This week he and Frank Sears were out tearing down and hauling Mr. Dole's burnt barn. Reginald had offered to build the new one, but the white construction company in town got the job.

Reginald had been forty when they married nine years ago. She'd been twenty-four, having almost resigned herself to spinsterhood. With her long jaw and small breasts she knew she wasn't the fetchingest peach in Farnsworth, though Reginald was all the time telling her otherwise.

Picking up her loaded basket, Lavonne noticed Lamar's kite drifting away, growing smaller and smaller.

"Oh, Lord," she sighed. Lamar must be heartbroke. It was only string and wood and paper, but knowing Lamar, he'd come home presently looking like his best friend had died.

It wouldn't hurt, she thought walking back to the small

white-and-green house, to bake a chocolate cake for after dinner. Lamar loved chocolate cake, and she wouldn't hear Reginald complaining either.

THE TAIL WAS THE ONLY COLORFUL THING ABOUT THE kite. Made of ribbons torn from rags and tied together the way his pa taught him, the tail delighted Lamar, and he thrilled at the complexities of the invisible breezes way up yonder that could drop a kite straight down, catch it, and scoot it left, then right.

"What you think, Hobo?" Lamar called. "Ain't it somethin'?"

The black-and-tan rat terrier, who knew the value of shade on a hot summer's day and who was holed up under a tangle of blackberry bushes, wagged his tail.

Suddenly, Hobo was on his feet in the sunlight, ears cocked toward the woods.

"What's the matter, Boy?"

And then he heard it too—the barking of a big dog.

Heading their way.

Lamar's hands shook as he reeled in his kite.

When Steven emerged from the woods into the meadow, Mauser was facing off with a rat terrier a fifth his size. Only where Mauser's tail stuck straight out behind him twitching snake-like as he growled, the runt's tail was wagging. The little dog was either stupid or incredibly brave.

Skeeter and Lance were already on the scene, egging Mauser on. A boy, maybe eight, dressed only in a pair of cutoff blue jeans, ran up with a stick. Steven saw a kite string drift by and tasted a metallic tang of danger in the air.

"I wouldn't shake that stick at my dog, if I were you!" hollered Billy Bob as he came huffing up, his blue eyes looking small and mean.

"Yeah, Mauser don't like nobody shaking sticks at him," Skeeter put in.

The boy ignored Skeeter, addressed Billy Bob: "Make him leave Hobo alone. We ain't done nothin' to you."

"You make him stop," Lance goaded. "You got the stick."

The terrier sniffed Mauser, and the Doberman bit the pooch on the nose. The terrier squealed, but instead of running away when it pulled free, it puffed out its chest and barked in Mauser's face.

The Doberman launched into the terrier, jaws clamping onto Hobo's shoulder, teeth ripping flesh in a series of rapid-fire bites, small hazel eyes as savage and cold as a shark's. The terrier yelped and defended itself by rolling over on its back and kicking and clawing the bigger dog in the face. But the Doberman got a hind leg in his jaws and slashed through muscle and tendons.

Everybody—except Billy Bob and Whitey—was shouting: Skeeter and Lance egging Mauser on; Steven and Jimmy yelling for Billy Bob to do something; the boy sobbing and hollering, "Stop! Stop!" as he whacked Mauser with the stick. Billy Bob was still smiling. Whitey stood with his hands covering his mouth, his eyes huge.

Then Mauser's fangs slashed into Hobo's throat, and the little dog slumped to the ground. Its eyes rolled up in its head as blood pooled on the grass.

"Holy shit!" Skeeter said, and they all stepped back, horrified.

Numb with shock, Steven saw the boy break his stick over Mauser's snout. Saw Mauser turn, snarling, knock the boy down and fasten his jaws on his throat. Saw Jimmy rush forward, yelling, tears in his eyes, only to be held back by Skeeter and Lance. Blood flew as the fangs released the throat and burrowed into the boy's belly. Blood flowered redly as the boy let out a gurgling scream that died as he choked.

Jimmy was crying; Skeeter licked his bottom lip as if caught between terror and fascination; Whitey was on his knees, retching.

Then Steven was running away from the horror and he was back under the sun-dappled canopy of the trees, pursued by images of a yellow-eyed monster pulling smoking entrails out of a dying boy and of red blood on green grass.

FOUR

S heriff Luther Wilcox glared across the kitchen table at his son, not quite believing what he was hearing. But there was no mistaking the ashen look on the boy's face.

"Billy Bob," he said, his anger heating him from the inside, turning his face red, "you sure he's dead?"

Billy Bob's head bobbed like the red-and-white float on a fishing line.

"Yes, sir, Pa. He was all tore up."

Luther—who had been a highly decorated Marine sergeant in Korea and had seen scores of men "all tore up" and who had "waded through blood and bodies," as he liked to brag to the boys out at the Red Rooster—reflected that Billy Bob's opinion as to what was dead and what might just look dead didn't amount to doodly-squat.

"Christ shit, Boy!" Luther said, a vein throbbing in his bull neck. "And you didn't try an' stop him?"

Billy Bob shifted uneasily and avoided his eyes.

"Don't you know reelection's comin' up this fall?" Luther added.

Billy Bob gulped but didn't answer.

"Look at me when I'm talkin' to you!" Luther slapped the Formica-topped table hard enough to knock the pepper shaker on its side. His eyes, blue as Billy's, had lost the smiling twinkle that had helped him get elected. They had darkened and grown cold, so that the only warmth left in them was from his anger. "What do you think people'll do if they hear the Sheriff's son sicced his dog on some poor rug rat?"

"But I didn't sic Mauser on him," Billy whined. "He just went crazy when the boy hit him."

Luther leaned across the table and slapped his son. Billy rubbed his cheek, blinked back tears. Angry as he was, Luther was pleased to see that the boy held them.

"Don't you whine, Son. You ain't no goddamned girl, are you?"

"No, sir." Billy Bob looked him in the eye and sat up straight.

Luther snorted. "Remember, Billy Bob, there's only two kinds a critters in this world—lions and sheep. And by God, I ain't raised no sheep!" He let his diamond-hard glare linger on Billy Bob a long moment to underscore what he'd said.

"No, sir," Billy said. "You ain't raised no sheep." But Luther didn't think he sounded particularly lionish.

All tore up...

"How 'bout these friends of yours? Think they all ran home and told their pas?"

Billy shook his head. "No, sir. I told 'em if anybody talked I'd sic Mauser on 'em."

"You did, huh?"

"Yes, sir."

Despite his anger, it warmed Luther's heart to think of other boys cowed by his son. Perhaps there was hope for the boy yet.

"Come on." Luther's chair scraped the plank floor as he rose. "You're gonna take me to the body, and if the boy's dead, you're gonna help me get rid of the body. And," he added as Billy Bob rose from the table and hurried after him, "you better pray we get to him first."

As Billy Bob and his friends had earlier, they approached the meadow through the woods, avoiding the road and the sharecropper shanties that sprouted alongside it like weathered toadstools.

Shifting the canvas tarp he carried on his shoulder, Luther glanced at his watch. The crystal was clouded inside from the humidity; tiny pearls of sweat clung to the forest of hair on his forearm. 4:18 p.m. Nearly two hours had passed since the mauling.

Coming out of the trees, squinting against the glare of the sun, Luther scanned the broad, tree-ringed meadow. He wondered what he would find. He couldn't make up his mind which would be better for him: if the boy had survived and made his way home (it'd be his word against Billy's) or if the boy was dead.

"Where?" he said impatiently. Though the meadow

appeared empty, there was no telling when somebody might blunder in. Maybe even the boy's parents looking for their son.

"Over yonder." Billy Bob pointed toward one of several thorny blackberry patches that dotted the meadow.

Not wasting time, Luther hurried toward the thicket, Billy Bob running to keep up. Luther noted the buzzing noise as they neared. It was a bad sign; the buzzing was too loud to be made by a few flies sampling a lump of dog shit.

He slowed as he neared the blackberry patch. He had been hunting since his pa first took him along when he was seven and he knew a thing or two about tracking; but he didn't have to be a tracker to see how the grass was trampled: here a sneaker tread, there a clear impression of a bare foot. He had left home the heavy black rubber-soled shoes he wore on duty and had changed into a pair of old sneakers, the tread of which was all but worn away. The sneakers would go out on the next garbage pickup. He didn't want to leave a trail leading to his door.

He was pleased at the confusion of the prints. It'd take a professional tracker to sort them out—and one wouldn't be called in just for the death of a poor sharecropper's boy. Luther made it a point to rake his foot across every halfway clear print he saw.

The body was a nightmare. The glazed terror-filled eyes stared up at the hot afternoon sky. A rope of intestine lay outside the gaping abdominal wound. Blood mudded the earth around the corpse. The stench was gagging. Flies lifted off the carcass in a dense cloud when Luther waved the tarp over them.

Billy Bob looked ready to pass out.

"It's about time you got yourself exposed to the more unpleasant aspects of life, Boy. Yeah, you seen dead rabbits and road-killed deer and you went to your Uncle William's funeral, but it ain't the same, is it, Boy?" He clamped his free hand on the back of Billy's neck when he started to look away.

"Conquer your fear now and you'll be better prepared to deal with it next time. You ain't gonna shame me and puke on your shoes, are you?"

Billy Bob shook his head, but he didn't look exactly certain.

Luther flapped the tarp. It settled over the corpse like a bedsheet. Then he leaned over, lifted the body by tucking the tarp in underneath it, set it on its side on a clean patch of grass and rolled it up, tucking the ends before completing the final fold.

"Shoulda brought a hank of rope," he said as he hefted the bundle onto his shoulder.

SPANISH MOSS HUNG LIKE TATTERED SHAWLS FROM the tall cypress trees, adding to the atmosphere of gloom and damp decay beneath the dense green canopy.

"So the dogs'll lose our track," Pa had said when Billy asked him why they'd driven around to another part of the woods when they could've reached the swamp faster from the meadow. Pa was smart like that. And he had guts too. He hadn't flinched when he'd hefted the tarp into his shoulder.

Trudging along behind Pa, poking the creek bottom with a stick for quicksand, even though he walked in Pa's footsteps, Billy had time to realize the sick feeling in his guts—like the feeling the flu left you with after twenty-four hours of puking and crapping—was caused by fear. His thudding heart felt empty—a cold, hollow space like a grave waiting for something to be buried.

"There it is," Pa said, and Billy looked up from his sand poking.

The white lightning scar ran the length of the dead cypress. The ancient tree rose on a small weed-choked hillock around which the shallow waterway forked. Pa, poking the ground before him, slowed as he entered the narrow right-hand fork.

Pa stopped. Billy Bob came up and peered around him. The creek ahead, flanked on either side by arching roots that overgrew the banks, looked no different than the creek behind them.

"Quicksand," Pa said.

The swamp air, sweltering to begin with, became unbearably claustrophobic as Billy inched forward, probing the earth with his stick. Gnats got in his eyes and mosquitos helped themselves to his blood. Suddenly, the end of Billy's stick disappeared. He froze, shivered from the chill that swept through him.

Pa came up beside him, and, swinging the body off his shoulder, unrolled the tarp so the body splashed into the murky water ahead of where Billy's stick had gone under. Luthor dragged the tarp back upstream and began swishing it around to wash the blood off. "No use leaving incriminating evidence," he said as casually as if he was scouring a frying pan.

The body sank slowly—too slowly for Pa. "Push him under," the sheriff said. "Use your stick."

Lamar's corpse had landed face down, for which Billy was thankful since it hid the boy's wounds. But he remembered the flies lifting off the body and his scalp crawled as he pressed the stick into the boy's back. The quicksand took its sweet time receiving the body. Billy kept pressing, terrified he would slip and fall into the quicksand with Lamar. The legs went under first. After that, the body sank quickly, like a battleship going under in a war picture.

The sand settled, the water cleared and once again reflected the dappled light. Billy Bob dropped the limb.

A grin hooked across Pa's face. "How do you feel, Son?"

"Like I'm gonna be awful sick."

Pa seemed to consider that. "That's okay, so long as you don't." Pa put his hand on Billy's shoulder and pressed so hard it felt like his collar bone was going to pop. Though it hurt like the dickens, Billy forced himself not to flinch.

"You know, Billy Bob," Pa said in that voice that always made the sweat on Billy's back turn to ice water, "I like being sheriff a whole lot. And I intend to get reelected." The grip tightened. Pa looked dangerous, his eyes all flinty and his jaw clenched, his blond Marine-cut bristling. And suddenly Billy was more afraid than he'd ever been in his life.

"If I lose my job," Pa said, "your little friend there's going to have company. There's plenty of room for the both of you. Understand?"

FIVE

Suppertime had come and gone and now the sun was fading and Lamar still hadn't come home. Lavonne Little was worried.

Reginald had come home dirty, ravenous, and dog-tired. Lavonne told him about the kite while he ate his supper of black-eyed peas, salt pork, and biscuits. "I'll make him another," Reginald had said, and then he'd smiled and nodded to himself as he always did when he had one of his ideas. "Remind me to bring home the Sunday funnies this weekend."

She'd felt better about the kite after that, but another hour passed and she woke Reginald dozing on the couch.

"He ain't home yet, Reg."

The springs of the ancient couch groaned as Reginald sat up and ran a broad, callused hand over his greying hair. "A boy's gonna miss supper now an' then. Best get used to it. Fact, I seem to rec'lect him bein' late to supper once or twice."

Which was true. Lamar often lost track of time in the

meadow blowing dandelions and waiting for the fireflies to come out. But here it was past eight o'clock, daylight, but just barely: the sky still blue, but shadows plentiful in the woods across the field.

Reginald rummaged in the kitchen for a flashlight, then said, "Come on, let's go find him." He was smiling, but she thought he didn't look as confident as before.

"Probably waitin' for the fireflies to come out."

"Most like."

THE SHADOWS WERE PURPLE UNDER THE PINES. Moments later, they emerged from the trees.

"Yonder, I reckon." She pointed to her right. "The kite was way up over those trees down the end of the meadow."

The mosquitos were out and they buzzed Lavonne, but she paid them no mind as her ears perceived a more sinister drone. As they pushed through the grass and dandelions, her attention was drawn to a mess of blackberry bushes not far ahead. Suddenly, she felt sick to her stomach and so dizzy her knees wobbled.

"Reg, do you think...?"

"Wait here."

Bad back or not, Reginald plowed through grass and ferns, making for the blackberry patch. A sob welled in her throat. *Knowing* before *seeing* it was going to be bad, she hurried after.

A whimpering noise rattled out of Reginald's mouth as he

stopped. Lavonne came up beside him. In the fading light, it took her a moment to recognize the small carcass lying in the trampled grass.

"Why it's Hobo," Reginald said, his voice trembling with relief. "My God."

The dog's wounds bristled with flies. Dark dew stained the grass. Hobo looked as if some wild animal had been at him. Lavonne, overcome by the sight and smell of death, stepped away from the carnage.

"Oh, my Lord!" Reginald said, looking at something in the grass nearby.

She followed Reginald's gaze, saw what he saw.

Lavonne moved in a stupor, pulse soaring, her hearing keen. That buzzing again. *Oh God no!* Her feet were lead. Her wobbling ankles threatened to topple her. The smell... She covered her mouth with her hand. Tears blurred her vision. Blotted out the sight of a second carnage.

TJ RILEY WAS CRUISING SOUTH ON PEABODY ROAD IN one of Farnsworth's two patrol cars, figuring on checking on Sue Ann and the girls before heading back into town and dreaming about trading in his rattling 1949 station wagon on the brand new 1956 Pontiac Star Chief convertible he'd seen on the lot over in Caledonia—green with green-tinted windows and buff interior and fat white walls—when a man lurched out of the woods into the circles of his high beams, flagging him down. The patrol car screeched to a stop inches from his legs.

"Thank the Lord!" the barrel-chested, grey-haired man said as TJ piled out.

"You old fool! Don't you know you can get yourself killed jumping out in front of a car like that!" TJ recognized him— Reginald Little, who'd done his driveway and patched the foundations when he and Sue Ann bought the house on Persimmon. Clutching one hand to his chest, Little heaved for breath. TJ hoped he wasn't about to have a stroke.

"What's wrong, Mr. Little?"

"Lamar! My boy!" the man gasped. "I think he hurt bad! You come, Mr. TJ."

LUTHER WAS MAD ENOUGH TO SNAP HEADS OFF WHEN he arrived at the meadow the second time that day. He'd had to leave his patrol car on the dirt tractor road that ran along-side a cornfield and walk in.

He'd been having a couple burgers at the Roller Burger, where pretty waitresses on skates brought your order, when TJ called in for a search party.

A search party!

Damn fool boy had been deputy for less than a year, but that didn't excuse his lack of judgement or his impertinence!

The gibbous moon, a couple slices shy of full, bathed the meadow in an ashen light as Luther came out of the trees.

He'd heard the group before he saw them: about ten men and a couple womenfolk milling about near the dark, humped mass of a blackberry patch, mumbling in sober tones

In his brown-and-tan uniform, TJ stood out like a pig in a dog pound as he left the group and hurried over.

"Did you bring rope, Luther?"

"What for?" Luther growled.

"To cordon off the area." TJ pointed back toward the crowd and the berry patch.

"'To cordon off—'?" Luther's face darkened. "Thomas Jefferson Riley, come here!" Luther thrust his face into the young deputy's, as he'd done to the hundreds of recruits he'd trained or led into combat. His eyebrows formed an angry V above his pug nose.

"Something wrong, Luther?"

"You called in for a search party?" Luther shouted point-blank into his face.

"Yes."

TJ sounded properly subdued; Luther backed off an inch. "Who gave you the power to authorize a search party? I thought that was my job."

"Luther, we got a boy missing here. We think he's dead."

"We?"

"Me—I."

Luther resumed walking toward the group of waiting moonlit faces. TJ fell into step beside him.

"The body's there?" Luther asked.

"No, that's why I wanted the search party."

"Looks like you got a search party."

"Neighbors."

Luther looked the group over: a few blacks, a smattering of whites, no townies, all local country folk gathered to perform a task that transcended racial barriers: to find a missing child. On the downside, Luther reflected, they probably all knew their way around the swamp. On the bright side, with all of their wandering around they were royally mucking up whatever tracks he might have missed.

"Why do you think he's dead if you ain't seen the body."

"Because of the blood, Sheriff."

A tall, horse-faced woman and a stooped old man with a woebegone face stepped away from the crowd, headed his way. Both of them carried flashlights. The beams played over the grass.

"Mrs. Little," TJ introduced. "The missing boy's mother. Reginald Little, his pa." The weathered expression on the man's lined face was not unlike expressions Luther had seen on the faces of GIs suffering from combat fatigue. The woman looked more resilient. Her expression was a mixture of terror and determination. She looked like she was holding herself together by a sheer act of will: she wasn't giving up on the son Luther knew for a fact was as dead as a doorknob.

"Hey, you! Get away from there!" Luther shone his light in the face of a strapping youth who was gridding the ground around the blackberry patch with a flashlight. "Show me," he said to the woman.

The blood was a dark stain under their collective lights. Luther saw one of his own footprints in the blood and stepped on it; then he examined the dog, which he hadn't bothered with that afternoon. Mauser'd done a job on it all right. The carcass buzzed with flies.

"What makes you think that's your boy's blood?" Luther asked.

"Whose else could it be?"

"What if the dog was killed over there and flung over here?" Luther pointed at the rat terrier's remains.

"Look, Sheriff," Reginald Little said. "I don't want to believe that's Lamar's blood. Nobody kin lose that much blood 'n' live. But all I want right now is to find my boy."

Which brings us back to the search party. Luther looked at the youth holding his flashlight close to the ground, squinting at the grass. The rest of the group were milling about trampling the ground. *Not a bad idea*, he thought.

Astonished, TJ watched Luther spread the men out in a loose line and then march his rag tag troops around the blackberry patch.

IN THE LIGHTLESS DEPTHS OF THE QUICKSAND HOLE, Lamar's corpse was not alone.

The skeleton, on top of which Lamar had settled, was that of an adult male. In life, the flesh that had clothed the man's bones had been a dark sun-kissed brown and the face that masked the skull had been handsome.

Unlike the boy's vacant husk, the Dark Man's soul was still with his mortal remains, fettered by words of power and a witch's will even as the skeleton was fettered by the iron plowshare roped to its chest. Despite his death and long incarceration, the man had continued to commune with the dark powers.

Lacking the sacrifices he had offered in life, he had offered promises.

Someone, it seemed, had been listening.

SIX

Sheriff Wilcox and that whiskey-nosed deputy of his, Mr. Seed, showed up back of the Littles' house at the crack of dawn with a big Doberman Pinscher and insisted on leading the search party even though her Uncle Lemus had showed up with four of his best coon hounds. Lemus and Reginald came back around noon tired and disappointed, saying how the Doberman had lost the scent.

Lavonne spent the morning stooped over, searching the woods foot by foot for Lamar's footprints, drops of blood— anything that might tell he was alive or where he'd gotten off to. But the ground was so thoroughly trampled that whatever trail there might have been was obliterated. If he'd owned a thimbleful of brains, she would have thought Luther Wilcox had churned up the ground on purpose; but she had recognized him last night for what he was—a prejudiced, pigheaded son-of-a-bitch who cared only for votes. If it had been the mayor's son, they'd have found the boy by now.

Before Reginald and Lemus went back out to conduct

their own search with Lemus' coon hounds, she overheard Reginald say to Lemus, if the hounds couldn't pick up the scent, they should search all the wells in the area. That could take days and the thought of what they might find sent shudders through her soul.

THAT AFTERNOON SHE WALKED INTO TOWN TO confront the sheriff.

Three marksmanship trophies and a citation for outstanding service adorned a shelf behind Luthor Wilcox. The fan in the one window of the small pine-paneled office ticked monotonously.

"What'd you want me to do? Fingerprint the blackberry bush?" the sheriff said, leaning back in his oak swivel chair. His tone was condescending, his expression annoyed.

Lavonne leaned forward, placed her hand on the desk. "You could, at least, send a sample of the blood to the State Police."

Luther slapped his desk. Lavonne flinched but didn't retreat. The man's eyes were round with anger, his lips compressed as if he with suppressed rage. The circles under his eyes confessed to a sleepless night. She had no idea why he was so angry, but she took it personally. She hadn't voted for him, still it was his duty to find Lamar.

"I'm tired of folks telling me how to do my business," he half-growled. "And, for your information, I already took care of that. Should have the report back by tomorrow. Happy?"

"You a hard man, Sheriff Wilcox. My son missin', maybe hurt bad—maybe dead—an' you ask me if I'm happy. You got no sympathy. Would you be happy if your boy was missin'?"

"Look, Mrs. Little—" The sheriff spread his palms on the desk as if he were smoothing wrinkles out of a tablecloth. "Normally, we wait forty-eight hours before we consider a person missing. We only started the ball rolling because of the blood. And we don't know yet if that blood is even human. Now, if there's nothing else I can help you with..." He glanced toward the door.

Lavonne choked back the urge to reach across the desk and slap the man's face. If she did, she figured her chances of getting tossed in jail were pretty good. And she was anxious to get home and help in the search.

Who knows, she thought. *Maybe they've found him. Lord, please let my baby be well.*

"I won't waste any more of your time, Sheriff," she said rising; "I sure you got lots more 'portant things to do than chewing the fat with a..." She didn't say the N-word, let it hang there between them.

Wilcox reddened. "I don't have to take that," he said, surging up from his desk, his bulk sending his swivel chair skidding backwards. He was around the desk faster than she would have thought possible, and she was backing away. Then he had her by the arm, his fingers prying into her flesh, and she was backpedaling on the balls of her feet to avoid the pain. Then she was out the door and the door slammed behind her.

Avoiding the eyes of Mr. Seed and the plump blond at the radio, Lavonne hurried through the outer office.

Sheriff Wilcox a dangerous man, she thought as she emerged into the glaring sunlight.

She paused on the sidewalk until the trembling passed. Then seeing town folk eyeing her standing in front of the Sherriff's Office like a goose in a duck pond, she hurried away.

SEVEN

Steven squinted up at the white-hot sunlight glittering down through the willow fronds on himself and Jimmy and Whitey. They sat on the roots of the big willow tree dangling their feet in the creek. *Twenty-four hours ago, the sun was right where it is now, staring down on the meadow. And it was happening.*

Steven remarked on the fact and Jimmy and Whitey squinted up through the arching branches at the sun.

"Twenty-four hours." Whitey shook his head. He was paler than usual; grey circles under his eyes mirrored Steven's own. "Seems like a week."

"Or a few minutes," Jimmy said. His gaze followed a twig floating downstream.

"Yeah." Steven knew the feeling. Coming home yesterday as late as he could without getting a tanning, he had soaked in a steaming bath till he got some color in his face. Then he'd spent a couple hours staring at TV with Mom and Dad and his little brother Mikey, but seeing, over and over, the terror and shock on the boy's face, the loop of bloody intestine glistening in the sun. He'd been glad it was the night for "Gunsmoke" and not Uncle Miltie; he wasn't sure he could have faked laughter. When he'd gone to bed, his private movie continued in the dark.

Gator, Steven's snow-white pit bull, drowsing in a sunny patch of grass on the bank, twitched her pink nose, stretched, yawned, and went back to drowsing.

"Geez," Steven said to Jimmy. "Do you really think Billy Bob told his pa?"

Jimmy shrugged and swept a black curl from his tall forehead. "You heard what Billy Bob said. He didn't say it outright, but his meaning was pretty clear."

Jimmy referred to the meeting Billy Bob had called this morning. They'd met at the picnic tables on the school playground—himself and Jimmy and Whitey and Lance and Skeeter and Billy Bob and Mauser. Billy Bob had kept it short and sweet, simply repeating his threat to sic Mauser on anyone squealing. But when Jimmy told Billy Bob he wasn't afraid of him or Mauser, Billy had said, "If you ain't afraid of Mauser, then you'd better be afraid of my pa!"

"What I don't get," Steven said, "is how come he wasn't where he died? He didn't get up and walk off after he was dead, did he?"

Whitey shivered. "Somebody moved him," he whispered.

"Yeah, and another thing," Jimmy added, "Billy Bob looked scared."

That he had, Steven reflected. Not all the sweat that had streaked his broad face this morning had been from the heat.

"Real scared. And the only person I can think of who could put that kind of fear into Billy Bob Wilcox is his pa."

"Yeah," Whitey said. "Billy Bob gets away with a lot of stuff, but I bet when he gets a stroppin' he really gets a stroppin'."

Whitey's preoccupation with stroppings was long standing. His parents were notorious scrappers and Whitey generally got caught in the middle of it. Whitey had once told him and Jimmy, after a particularly severe stropping, that he'd asked his mother why she'd whupped him and she'd said it was because "Little boys have such *dirty* minds." Steven remembered the way Whitey had screwed up his face imitating his mother when he'd said the word *dirty*.

Steven sighed.

"What's the matter, Blankenship?" Jimmy said.

Calling him by his last name was Jimmy's way of showing concern. Steven spread his hands, looked at Jimmy, at the water. "I feel so guilty that I ran yesterday. I keep thinking that if I hadn't been such a scaredy-cat, I could have helped you and maybe the kid would still be alive."

Jimmy spun a piece of bark into the creek, shook his head. "I wanted to run away, too."

"Why didn't you?"

Jimmy was thoughtful for a moment, then he said, "My pa once told me a story about when he was a kid and two bullies wanted to beat him up. He said he had two choices: fight or run. He figured if he ran, they would just get him next time; so he punched the bigger boy in the Adam's apple." Whitey put his hand to his own prominent Adam's apple and looked uncomfortable. "The other bully ran away and neither one of 'em ever bothered him again. So yesterday I just thought, 'What would Pa do?'" Jimmy shrugged. "Pa ain't the running type; I guess I ain't either."

"I guess that makes me the running type," Steven said.

"And me the pukin'," Whitey said sheepishly.

MRS. WALLACE, THE NEIGHBOR WHO CLEANED AND cooked for him and his pa, had left Billy Bob a plate of food covered with tinfoil on the kitchen table. Normally, Billy loved Mrs. Wallace's cooking, but now the breaded drumsticks were cemented to the plate with congealed grease and the mashed potatoes were as stiff as drying plaster, solidifying into the pinnacled shape into which Billy Bob had molded them.

Billy was hungry, but his head throbbed and his stomach was sore from a night of diarrhea. He pushed the plate to the center of the table, covered it with the tinfoil. The sight of the food made him see again the flies swarming in the boy's pulpy wounds.

He kneaded his eyes with the heels of his hands, heard distinctly the sullen and terrifying splash Lamar's body had made when Pa dumped it into the water. Billy's chair scraped as he pushed back from the table and went out on the porch where he wouldn't have to smell fried chicken and where, maybe, the bright sunshine would keep the squirming visions away.

Out back—far enough from the house so the breeze wouldn't carry the stink into the kitchen—a long-abandoned chicken coop baked in the sun. After Korea, before he decided to run for sheriff, Pa had tried his hand at chicken farming.

Billy vaguely remembered scooping the seed out of the barrels and throwing it to the chickens in double handfuls—and getting his hide tanned when Pa caught him. "Chickens'll eat till they bust, Billy Bob!" he remembered Pa telling him. Despite Pa's efforts, the cholera had taken them.

Billy sat on the top step and wished his ma hadn't run off. Not that he blamed her—Pa's temper could be scary. But she had held him and had encouraged him to talk to her—things Pa never did.

A vague recollection—an image—of his mother flying across the kitchen after Pa hit her. He also recalled the occasional bruise or black eye. Ma had known better than to argue with Pa, but she had done it anyway. Billy thought that he would never argue with Pa. It hurt enough when Pa stropped him; he shuddered to think what it would feel like if Pa punched him.

Don't you know reelection's comin' up this fall?

Billy Bob grinned nervously and scraped the splintery back step with the heel of his sneaker. If he screwed up Pa's reelection, a knuckle sandwich would be the least of his worries. He hoped his threat worked and that Pa never found out that he'd mentioned him to the others.

There's plenty of room for the both of you, Billy thought and shivered.

EIGHT

The moon slipped in and out of clouds. Lavonne was thankful for its light as she made her way through the pines. She had come alone because it was commonly held that the hoodoo woman didn't like menfolk. Besides, Reginald was bone-tired and heartsick from searching.

The katydids were shrill in the surrounding trees, and from the swamp ahead pulsed a chorus of croaking frogs. Together, the insects and amphibians presented a wall of sound as loud and ceaseless as the bailing machine that sometimes ran all night over at Mr. Lamont's farm, its noise carrying across the fields.

A cloud slid over the moon and she picked her way more slowly until the light returned. She should have come during the day, she knew; but she'd clung to the hope that one of the searchers would find Lamar lost in the woods or sleeping in a haystack and bring him home unharmed—or, at the worst, maybe with a sprained ankle or a broken leg.

Please Lord, please let it be nothing worse than a broken leg, she prayed.

But she knew it was worse—much worse. As much as she wanted to believe Lamar would come walking in the door, she couldn't ignore her intuition. Lamar had met with violence.

Then why hadn't she heard him screaming?

Did you scream, baby? Did you call for me and I didn't hear you?

Oh Lord, please let my baby be alive! Lord, please let me find him!

Hot tears streaked her face.

It occurred to her that whoever or whatever killed Hobo and attacked Lamar might be out here, but she would welcome an encounter. She carried a hefty three-foot length of branch she'd picked up especially for that purpose. Nevertheless, she was afraid—more afraid of what Mrs. Flowers might tell her than of anything she might run into in the woods.

Overhead, a bat, caught for a second in a web of moonlight, flapped by, vanished into shadows.

Behind her, a twig snapped.

Lavonne turned with her club held at the ready but saw nothing but vague tree shapes.

A scuffing sound, like a hoof scraping against pebbles. In spite of the club and her desire to meet face to face whoever or whatever had taken Lamar, fear spread through her like a serpent's cold venom.

Footsteps now, moving toward her.

Oh my God!

She turned to run, tripped over a root and fell hard on her hands and forearms.

A foot tread, rushing over pine nettles.

She turned, raising her stick to ward off her attacker.

A black silhouette loomed over her. The moon emerged from a cloud.

Her scream stopped in her throat.

"Reginald!"

Her husband reached for her, helped her up. "You all right, Lavonne?"

"I was until you scared the bejesus out of me!"

"Damn, woman." He dusted her off. "When I saw you were gone and I looked out and saw you heading into the woods, first thing I thought was whatever killed...Hobo...might be out here tonight. I ain't ready to lose you too, Lavonne."

Lavonne sagged against Reginald's broad chest. "Oh, Reg," she sobbed, her face wet with tears, "I want my baby."

"Me, too," Reginald moaned into her hair. "Me, too."

SOMEBODY COMIN'.

Mauvis Flowers, the hoodoo woman, stood on her porch and sniffed the air. She'd known all day somebody would be visiting—and not just for the usual gallbladder or rheumatism remedy or her honey or homemade jams either. She'd read the signs.

First, the morning glories that covered the porch rail hadn't opened. Though it had been a typically hot July day, much the same as yesterday and the day before, they had remained closed all day. Then there were the bats. Seemed like every bat in the county had gathered hereabouts, flitting in and out of the pine and oak fringe of the swamp. Then the bullfrogs had started up. There were always lots of frogs in the swamp, but never in her life had she heard such chorusing.

The signs weren't hard to read: they all spelled trouble. And unless it was the earth itself fixing to split open and gobble her up, trouble usually meant people.

A crow cawed in the night, close by a jay complained. Her visitors were near.

LAVONNE FOUND MRS. FLOWERS' ONE-ROOM CABIN not at all the filthy witch's den she had imagined since girl-hood. The house was clean, the simple hand-hewn pine furnishings and cedar chest at the foot of the bed well-oiled. The room would have been comfortable—were it not for the excessive heat. Despite it being a hot July night, a fire blazed in Mrs. Flowers' hearth, making the cabin stifling. Judging from the deep orange-glowing bed of embers, Mrs. Flowers had been burning logs for hours. The aroma of burning cedar filled the cabin. One window was open, letting in the noise of the croaking bullfrogs and a draft that was sucked across the floor into the fire.

"You brought something of his with you?" asked the hoodoo woman seated at the table opposite Lavonne. Reginald had been ordered to wait on the porch.

Lavonne reached into one of the big front pockets of her

house dress and drew out a small white tee shirt. "He wore this to bed night before last.

The old woman took the cotton shirt and examined it under the kerosene lantern that hung over the table. In its yellow glow, Mrs. Flowers' face shone like oiled mahogany. Sitting close to her, Lavonne saw the delicacy of her skin; were it not for the grey hair tied neatly into a bun and the slight stoop in her shoulders, Lavonne might have taken her for a younger woman. There was a sadness in the old woman's light-brown eyes that mirrored the pain in Lavonne's heart.

Mrs. Flowers pressed her nose into the cotton shirt and inhaled deeply. "Yes, this will do." She rose and went to the tall pine rocking chair at the edge of the hearthstone. The chair would have been too close to the fire in the dead of winter; it was insensibly close tonight.

Seating herself, Mrs. Flowers took up a long hickory-wood staff and pushed the burning log off the iron grate so that only the deep bed of embers remained. Rocking slowly, sweat trickling down her face, she stirred the coals with her staff, embers flared bright yellow, sparks rushed up the chimney. Lavonne, who had come as close to the fire as she could bear, saw that the staff was charred at the end.

Continuing her slow rocking, Mrs. Flowers laid her staff across her knees and, fingering the tee shirt in her lap, stared into the heat.

"I see a face," she said. "A young boy—maybe eight or nine. Small, wearing blue short pants. He wears no shirt and is barefoot."

Lavonne's heart quickened. Amazed, she peered into the fire—and saw nothing but glowing embers. A caterpillar of supernatural fear crept up her damp spine; she didn't believe the woman was guessing.

The hoodoo woman rocked. Her feet, gnarled like the roots of an ancient oak and encased in worn leather sandals, pumped up and down. The soft creak of the rockers on the plank floor was as hypnotic as the heat patterns.

"The boy is smiling. There's a dog with him, a little dog...black and brown..."

"That's Hobo!"

"Shhh." Mrs. Flowers cocked her head and seemed to be listening intently to the flames.

"Now there's another dog. Big dog. Barkin' up a storm."

The old woman remained silent a moment, during which Lavonne thought, *A big dog*. So Sheriff Wilcox was right after a fashion: Hobo, and maybe Lamar too, had been attacked by a wild dog!

"I see other boys coming now. Five—no *six* of them." The hoodoo woman shook her head. "It's hard to see. Everybody's movin'. Some sort of fight goin' on. I see blood—red blood on green grass."

Lavonne could remain silent no longer. "Is Lamar alive? Is my boy alive?"

"No," Mrs. Flowers said without taking her eyes off the embers.

"My God!" Lavonne cried out and covered her face with a shaking hand.

Anger welled up inside her, pushing aside the tears; grief was replaced by a consuming hate. "Where's my boy now? Where have they hidden him?"

Mrs. Flowers was silent as she stared into the embers for a long while. Though her eyes were open, it was as if she'd fallen into a trance. Lavonne was about to repeat her question when the old woman shook her head. "I don't know. I get an impression of darkness and—" She drew her arms close to her as if shrinking from cold and stopped rocking. "—something pressing all around."

They've buried him! Lavonne thought, shocked. "Can you find him?"

Mrs. Flowers turned from the fire. Her forehead was deeply furrowed when she met Lavonne's gaze. The hoodoo woman shook her head. "No, but..."

"'But' what?"

"He might come to you."

Lavonne stared. "But you said—"

Mrs. Flowers nodded and took Lavonne's hands in hers. "I'm so sorry to be the one to tell you. Yes, I believe your son is dead."

"But you can bring him back?"

Mrs. Flowers waved her hand. "Forget I said anything. It's not something a Christian ought to dwell on."

"'Forget'? How can I forget?" Angry tears streaked Lavonne's face. "Mrs. Flowers, you don't know what it's like to lose your only child. Oh, my sweet baby!"

MAUVIS WAITED PATIENTLY, STRUGGLING WITH HER own tears as the woman was overcome with weeping. She looked into the woman's grief-lined face, but only for a moment, then returned her gaze to the fire, a lump in her throat, tears in her eyes; it was less painful by far to stare into the scarlet flames licking over the bed of embers than to gaze into the woman's eyes. The woman's fresh grief stirred Mauvis' old one.

Don't know what it's like to lose my only child! Sweet Jesus in Heaven, how wrong you are.

Even after thirty years, her grief was like an unhealed wound, the thin scab ready to open and bleed.

Tearfully, Mrs. Little dropped to her knees at Mauvis' side. "Please!" the younger woman beseeched. "You say my baby dead. Lord knows I don't want to believe you. But if he is, please don't deny him a decent Christian burial. Please... I want to see my baby again so bad! You just don't know what it's like!"

Mauvis trembled. The sight of this bereft mother on her knees pleading for the body of her dead babe tore down the wall she had built around her own sorrow as if it were a thing of clay melting under a torrential rain. Tears spilled, hot and salty, down her own cheeks. Her hands returned the woman's squeeze as much to give consolation as to receive it.

"It can be done," she said.

"Please bring him back." The woman's eyes were unwavering in their appeal.

"I'm not saying I can restore your son's life. Are you sure you want the dead knocking at your door?"

Mrs. Little paused to consider this, her eyes round and tear-swollen, the firelight emphasizing their redness. Then she was nodding, her gaze resolutely fixed on Mauvis.

"Yes, bring him back," she whispered, as if, Mauvis thought, this Christian woman realized the unholy implications of what she asked.

THE RITUAL WAS ANCIENT. HER GRANDMOTHER HAD taught it to her, along with the rest of the Knowledge. And it was simple—for someone with the Gift. The Gift and the Knowledge were essential. All she needed besides these was the Blood.

Mauvis held the glass before the ruddy embers and the inch of red liquid caught fire. Mrs. Little had pulled forty dollars from her yellow housedress and had tried to press it into her hand; but Mauvis had told her no, she wouldn't take her money, what she needed was blood.

The woman had stared into her eyes for a long moment as if deciding whether she was mad. Then she had gone over to her cupboard and had taken a knife and, without flinching, had deeply sliced the heel of her hand and held a glass under the trickling blood.

IN THE CRUSHING DARKNESS AT THE BOTTOM OF THE quicksand hole, the Dark Man lay in his new suit atop the scattered bones of his old. Anger and frustration burned in him. The urge to throttle a human throat, to feel the flesh yielding beneath his fingers, hadn't diminished in the decades he had moldered in the pit.

In spite of his new body and the fact that he was no longer bound, the quicksand fettered him as surely as had the iron plowshare. Like manna fallen from Heaven, he had access to movement but couldn't do a thing about it.

After a while, he quieted his anger and pondered what to do. He could call upon animals in the area to throw themselves into the pit and then climb up their corpses, but he reflected that he would get mostly fish and turtles and birds and anything as big as a stray cow he hesitated calling for fear that it might land on top of him and he'd never escape.

At a loss for alternatives, he lay there, raging and fuming at the one who'd put him there as he hadn't in decades, not since he'd woke and found himself dead and buried at the bottom of the quicksand hole with a plowshare tied to his chest.

Suddenly, a chill washed through him and he felt the contact of a distant mind. To his amazement, the carcass stirred and began hauling itself free of the bones, began dragging itself up the side of the pit, its hands and feet digging in, unfettered by the ponderous sand.

The cadaver smiled as the Dark Man realized what was happening: someone like himself—someone with the Knowledge—was summoning the corpse. Experiencing a wild exhilaration, he lent his will to the task.

NINE

Home again, Lavonne paced. And waited.

Now and again, she'd sit in the cane-backed chair and rock briskly with the mechanical discipline of a clock pendulum; then she'd get up and pace some more, all the while glancing nervously at the front door, at the tarnished brass knob, at the hook latch that was the door's only lock—the hook dangling now because Lamar was coming home.

Why then did she feel a powerful urge to walk over to the door and fasten the latch? Was it because the door might choose that moment to swing open and Lamar might be standing there?

Is Lamar alive? Is my boy alive?

No.

Lavonne wrung her hands. *Mrs. Flowers is wrong! Lamar can't be dead! He's just a baby, a little boy! He's got so much living to do! He still has to go to school, grow up and become a man!* She had thought so much on all the life stages that awaited—on seeing him as a skinny teenager and then as a tall, broad-shouldered man—much taller than Reginald or herself. Life without him was unthinkable.

Biting her thumb knuckle, her left hand clenched in a fist at her side, she wished she hadn't sent Reginald over to Mr. Lamont's to call Dr. Campbell.

"Mrs. Flowers said he would come to us and he may be in bad shape," she had told Reginald.

"'Come to us'? How's she gonna make him come to us?"

"Reginald... Go." She had waved her bandaged hand to cut off further comment. Reginald was a good Christian. The fact that he had gone with her to Mrs. Flowers' house meant that he was willing to go to extremes to find Lamar, but no use both of them risking their immortal souls. Better he never knew what she had begged of Mrs. Flowers.

The bare lightbulb dangling at the end of its wire with a pull string hanging down to switch it on and off went out, plunging the room into darkness.

Heart thumping, Lavonne made her way to the kitchen. Feeling around in the dark, she found the table and, reaching above it, found the string and pulled. She heard the *click* overhead, but no light was forthcoming. She found herself waiting for the dead in a dark house.

Not dead not dead not dead!

Feeling her way to the cast-iron wood stove, its metal cool to the touch, she took one of the long stick matches from the tin holder; then, making her way past the cupboard, took down the hurricane lantern that hung by the back door. Sliding a match under the glass, she lit the wick and dialed the flame up bright. Suddenly, she couldn't get enough light; she wished it were broad daylight and the roof gone.

A knock came at the front door.

It's not locked! she started to call, thinking Reginald was back, but caught herself.

"Lamar?" she said in a small voice. Her heart raced. Shadows capered like demons in the corners, slid like serpents over the walls, as—holding the lantern before her, its yellow glow a shield against the encroaching dread—she made her way into the front room.

Halfway to the door, where the braided straw rug lay before the tired couch, she froze as her nocturnal visitor knocked again: three hollow thumps, like the rap of the dead on the inside of a coffin. The hook latch dangled. The door-knob gleamed a dull expectant yellow.

The knob turned.

Lavonne didn't move as the door swung slowly inward and the lantern glow fell on the child standing on the threshold.

"Lamar!" she sobbed. Her arms reached for him, but something stayed her feet.

Lamar's face, his small body, his short pants, his bare feet were caked with wet sand that sloughed off him and spattered to the floor as he stepped into the room. Veins protruded from the hideous rent in his throat, and from the purpled night-mare of his belly, a loop of intestine hung over the waistband of his shorts. Even thus, dead and mutilated as he was, Lavonne would have embraced him. It was the eyes that stayed her. And the grin.

For every step Lamar took into the room, Lavonne took one back. And when he opened his mouth and quicksand bubbled out, she fainted.

THE DEAD THING LEAPED FORWARD, CAUGHT THE lantern from her hand as she fell. Carrying the light into the kitchen, he sat it on the table and, from a cabinet drawer he knew to be off limits to the boy, he withdrew a long, wicked-looking butcher knife. The Dark Man was pleased as he wielded the blade in his small but powerful grasp and admired the reflection of the lantern flame flickering along its length.

Back in the front room, the woman lay unconscious. Lamar stood over her spread-eagled form and bent to rip open the buttoned front of her house dress to get at the heart. Heart flesh gave him long life, and blood was needed for the ritual.

Footsteps outside. He cocked his ear. A heavy tread mounting the porch steps.

He hurried back into the kitchen, eased the door shut as boots entered the house.

"Wha—?" A man's voice. Sifting through the scattered memories left in the dead boy's brain, the Dark Man recognized it as Lamar's father. It was dark in there but the woman lay near the door, and, though the moon had set, there was enough starlight for the man to see.

A startled cry proved him right. A rush of work boots on the pine floor.

Drunk with savage anticipation, the Dark Man pressed his back against the wall, licked his lips, and waited.

"LAVONNE!"

Reginald dropped to his knees at her side, rolled her onto her back. She was unconscious but breathing. No blood or evidence of injury that he could see. Had she simply fainted?

The front door had been open. Of course, Lavonne probably left it open to let Lamar in. *But the sand...* Wet sand on the porch and on the floor. Sand that crunched under his shoes...

His eyes narrowed in his broad, lined face; his shoulders hunched as he leaned protectively over Lavonne. He scanned the dark room but saw nothing out of place. Except the sand. And a rank whiff as of swamp mud and meat gone over.

A light was on in the kitchen.

He rose, stepped away from Lavonne, reached up and pulled the light string. The room remained dark. He started for the kitchen, stopped, approached the hearth, and drew an iron poker rattling from the bucket. Hefting the weapon, his eyes narrowed suspiciously at every possible place of concealment as he made his way to the kitchen.

Light spilled through the widening crack as he pushed the door open. Tensing, he listened carefully before entering the room. A lighted lantern sat on the table. He paused to glance through the crack where the door was hinged to the wall to see if anyone was hiding there. No one was. He stepped inside.

Reginald, like anyone who works with his hands, had cut

himself many times in his various occupations as a handyman and farmer. Most cuts were insignificant, knicks that soon healed; but there was one time when he was sixteen and playing with his daddy's hunting knife, he'd cut his thumb pretty near to the bone. The sudden pain he felt in his right side just below the ribs was like that, hot and unnerving. Looking down, he saw the grinning face, the ragged ruin of the corpse's throat, the small hand gripping the handle of the butcher knife. A stench of corruption bloated up into his face, laced with a hot coppery whiff of blood.

"*Gotcha!*" croaked the thing that looked like Lamar but couldn't possibly be. With the nimbleness of a wild creature, the horror yanked the butcher knife out of his side and jumped out of range of the poker.

Reginald took a step toward the dead thing that had been his son and collapsed onto his knees.

"Lamar!"

Lamar's face was crusted with quicksand. Only—

The slit eyes...the leering mouth...

"You're not Lamar."

In reply, the creature reached out and drew the blade across Reginald's throat.

TEN

I Bloody Bones. I ridin' your bike an' I comin' to get you.

Lying in bed staring into the darkness, Lance tried to pinpoint the voice. It seemed to come through the open window from the yard below, yet it seemed to echo hollowly off the walls of his skull. The voice was that of a black man, but different than folks around Farnsworth. Lance had heard a man speak like that once in a pirate movie he'd seen at the Starlite drive-in.

And he did hear his bike, heard the *r-r-r-r-r* of the playing cards he'd stuck between the spokes.

Good! The noise would wake his parents. Dad would make the prankster go away.

But his parents didn't wake. The *r-r-r-r-r* of the cards went on for another minute, during which he heard no sound of shifting bedsprings through the wall, nor of his father's gruff complaining.

The bicycle stopped. Holding his breath, Lance strained to

hear over his booming heart. Then, like a serpent slithering in his brain, the voice.

I Bloody Bones an' I comin' to get you.

The back door opened and closed.

Oh my God! He's in the house!

Despite the warmth of the night, Lance shivered, his pajamas were soaked, his sheets damp. Fear oozed from his pores.

I Bloody Bones— The voice crawled like ants over the inside of his skull. *—I on the stairs an' I comin' to get you.*

Footsteps on the stairs!

Tom and Jerry, Lance's painted turtles, scrabbling frantically, kicked gravel against the glass of the fishbowl. Still no sound from his parents' room. He longed to bang on the wall, but fear kept him still.

I Bloody Bones. I in the hall an' I comin' to get you. You try to turn on your lamp, but it don' work.

Lance jumped. The thought of a lightless encounter spurred him into action. He reached out and clicked the chain hanging down under the lampshade. The room remained smothered in darkness.

The hall light goes out, the voice said. And the hall light did go out: the faint grey line at the bottom of his door went black.

The air in the room had grown thick and sluggish and pressed over his face like a pillow. A frenzy of activity in the fishbowl: sounded like Tom and Jerry were digging a tunnel.

The knob clicked, and in the darkness he saw the dim rectangle of the door swing slowly wide and the ebony shadow standing there.

Lance woke, his eyelids flinging open like window shades.

He opened his mouth but didn't have time to cry out before the plunging knife skewered his Adam's apple and, grating against vertebrae, buried its point in his pillow.

THE DARK MAN LOPED THROUGH THE CORNFIELD. He'd discarded the short pants the corpse had worn and the cornstalks raked his dead flesh. His tiny flaccid penis flopped against his thigh; entrails flapped in the distended flesh of his gut wound. The corpse would not know exhaustion—only the inevitable decay that was the lot of all things dead.

The moon had long set and he ran by starlight, thrilling in the exhilaration of movement after an eternity of confinement. Pebbles dug into his bare feet, but he didn't feel them; the air drafted against his unblinking eyeballs, but he felt nothing; the body was insensate. Rather, he recalled these things from his previous life as vividly as he remembered lust and the satiation of lust.

Gotcha!

He remembered saying that to the corpse's father, as the knife slid deliciously into the man's side. The word, along with images of a bleeding skeleton, he had found in the dead boy's brain, left behind like scattered belongings in his hasty departure. It was one of the boy's most recent memories. That and the image of a newspaper kite against a blue sky; and, of course, the powerful sensations of terror and pain and images of a snarling, biting dog; the flying droplets of red, glinting in the sunlight as they arched over the grass; the horror of ruptured flesh. The Dark Man found the images intoxicating.

Suddenly, the corpse's legs locked on him and he almost tumbled. Then the whole body was turning, as if directed by the will of another, and he felt a chill as cold as winter and damp as the swamp. Looking east, his gaze drawn as if by a magnet, he saw running along the tops of the trees a grey ribbon.

Dawn. He was seeing his first dawn in thirty years.

The corpse ran toward the woods, carrying him back to the swamp.

ELEVEN

I t is a whore of a morning. Only eight-thirty and already the sun beats down hot as bacon grease sizzling in a fry pan. Already the night's fog has burned off the swamp, deep in the woods where pine needle-carpeted earth gives way to water and bog. Mosquitos, gnats, and iridescent dragonflies buzz and swarm and dart in the bright sunlight arrowing down through the moss-hung cypresses. Save for an occasional caw of a crow circling over the fields beyond the woods and the indolent, constant buzz of insects, the only noise is the baying of hounds.

And the crunch of sand and pine needles beneath three pairs of boots.

Luther cursed under his breath and mopped his face with a big red handkerchief. The hounds were skittish and kept shying away from the track—which suited him just fine, considering the direction they were taking. But old Dewey McFarland and his son Jeb kept after them, cursing and yelling and whacking them when they turned back.

At least he'd had the presence of mind to switch the sample of blood TJ had taken from the crime scene for one of dog's blood. That should throw the Staties off the scent.

"Don't know what's got into 'em!" Dewey exclaimed, scratching his chin through his grizzled beard as Jeb forced the dogs on. He removed his red-and-white Tractor Supply cap and wiped his brow with a hairy forearm. The hounds hadn't lost the scent, they simply didn't want to pursue it— which was highly odd for Dewey's dogs; the Redbones up ahead were three of the best trackers in the county, and every one of them acted like he had a bee up his butt.

"You'd think they was trackin' Satan himself," Dewey growled and sniffed the air.

Luther figured Dewey's sense of smell was no keener than his own, and all he smelled was pine and earth and, now and again when a breeze stirred from the swamp ahead, mud and rot. Pretty soon they would come to a shallow, sandy-bottomed stream, and if the dogs bore left and headed deeper into the swamp they might come to the dead, lightning-scarred cypress and his secret.

What in blazes is going on? he wondered for the dozenth time that morning. Two homicides in one night. Both victims had contact with the deceased, Lamar Little, within the past two days. Child-size footprints had been plainly visible around both corpses, and traces of wet sand had been found at both crime scenes. To top it all off, the killer's track led a few miles through woods and meadows, then veered straight for the swamp.

The only one he knew who had cause to kill Lance Newcome was Lavonne Little. But that didn't make sense because her husband had also been murdered, and—besides the fact that her feet were too big to have made the childish footprints—when he'd arrived at the Littles' house, some of the womenfolk from the neighborhood had put Lavonne Little in her bed and had covered the husband, Reginald Little, with a blanket. When Luther had gone in to see the woman, she couldn't have looked more shell-shocked if a howitzer had gone off in her ear.

"Jumpin' Jesus," Dewey swore, shaking his head. "Whadya think the killer done with their hearts?"

Luther shrugged, scowled at the sun dazzling down through the pines. "Don't know."

"I'll tell you one thing," Dewey said, wagging a stubby index finger. He shot an amber stream of tobacco into the pine needles, "If'n you don't turn up a stranger, then it's got to be someone livin' hereabouts, mark my words."

"Well, whoever it is is about as sick as they come and needs to be put out of his misery. Know what I mean?" Luther patted his .38.

Dewey grinned and scratched his ear. "Yeah, I hear that."

A fierce yapping followed by a loud *yip* and a burst of canine whines interrupted their conversation. A hound had snapped at Jeb, and Jeb had kicked it under the chin so hard the dog had landed on its side. Looking beyond Jeb, Luther was jolted by the sight of sunlight glittering on water: the stream he and Billy Bob had waded day before yesterday.

Dewey and Jeb were practically wrestling with the dogs now. They had them down to the stream but the canines refused to go in.

"Let's head back, Dewey," Luther said. He didn't want to know which direction the dogs would head if they followed the scent, nor did he want Dewey or Jeb to know.

"But what about your killer? Don't you wanna catch 'im?"

"I will. Just let 'em go."

Dewey scowled at his dogs as if they were traitors; he looked shamed and angry. "Let 'em go, Jeb," he growled.

The gangling youth, who had just thrown one of the dogs into the stream and was about to toss another one, let the dogs creep guiltily past him.

"Go on!" Dewey yelled, kicking at one as it neared, ears down, head bowed, tail between its legs. The dogs took off running back the way they'd come. They didn't seem to have any problem running away from the scent.

"Animals sense things," Dewey said, squinting one eye into the sunlight. "Natural things and unnatural things. Know what I mean?"

"Dewey, what the hell you talkin' about?" Luther was in no mood for games.

"I'm jus' sayin' maybe the devil had a finger or two in these doin's."

Dewey nodded as if agreeing with himself and spat another stream of tobacco juice into the brush. He looked around at the trees as if someone might be listening, then said confidentially, "My guess is some sort of hoodoo ritual."

Luther didn't smile. Dewey had reminded him of something Lyle Hennes told him when he'd stopped by the office to call Dewey and to brief Hank Seed and TJ on the murders. The old jailkeeper said he recalled some murders that had taken place years ago. "Nineteen twenty-something or other. Before your time. I was workin' in the Post Office. From every body—the ones they found leastways—the heart was missing, ribs broken, arteries chopped." And then Lyle had offered the same theory as Dewey's.

"Hoodoo," Luther repeated.

Dewey nodded. "Yep, probably used the hearts to toast the devil's health. It's a fact a lot of these swamp folks hereabouts still believe in that mumbo jumbo stuff. You seen the way my dogs ran; ain't nothin' natural gonna make my dogs hightail it like that."

Luther conceded that Dewey had a point.

Back at the patrol car, Luther called in.

"'Lo, Connie," he called into the radio soon as he was seated.

"TJ here, Luther. Connie called in sick."

"She did, did she?" Connie usually called in sick one or two days every month. Plumbing problems, Luther assumed. "Tell her I hope she feels better." Once word about the murders got around—and get around it would—Connie would be calling in, cramps or no cramps. "Any calls?"

"Yeah. Mayor called."

"Yeah? What'd Hanley want?"

"Wants you to drop by his office. What's your 10-20? Over."

"Never mind my 10-20. My 10-19 is Hanley's. Give him a courtesy call and tell him I'm on my way. Another thing— Lyle still there? Over."

"Yeah, he's here. Over."

"Get Lyle to help you dig the old records out of the basement and call Mrs. Greentree over to the library and ask her to send over whatever she can find on those missing heart cases Lyle was blowin' about. Over."

TWELVE

"**A**re they going to send Aunt Lavonne up to Milledgeville, Granny Apple?" Mazy asked, fidgeting on the straight-back chair.

"Might." Granny Apple rocked as she cooled herself with a cardboard fan with a picture of the Lord's last supper on it that looked suspiciously like the fans kept in the backs of the pews at the Mount Zion Baptist Church along with the Bibles and hymnals. Nearly as thin as her walking stick, Granny Apple had been a widow for nearly fifteen years and had close to twenty grandchildren. She wasn't Mazy's granny though, nor was she Aunt Lavonne's. Granny Apple lived a short spell up the road and had established a long tradition—longer than Mazy had been on Earth and she was twelve—of visiting the sick and dying. "If she don' snap out of it," Granny Apple continued. "Mind you, I heard tell of people what just lay there starin' with they eyeballs ajumpin' like they was dreamin' for days or years, and then one day they jus wakes up."

Years... Mazy thought and shuddered, picturing Aunt Lavonne lying on her back in the Milledgeville loony bin. Just lying there and staring at the ceiling.

Mazy's mama, Rowena Johnstone, who sat by the window knitting by the afternoon light, dabbed a handkerchief at her red eyes. In stark contrast to Granny Apple, Mama was stoutly built, her wide hips filling up the comfortable stuffed chair. She and Aunt Lavonne (who was no more her aunt than Granny Apple was her granny) had been friends since girlhood. Mama had been crying all morning. "I don't think it's something we should talk about," Mama said. Her voice was quiet and sad.

"'The Lord giveth and the Lord taketh away,'" Granny said consolingly.

"Amen," Mama said and looked out the window, her needles observing a moment of rest.

"Amen," Mazy whispered.

Granny Apple blew her nose. "Frogs sure loud last night," she said as she returned the Kleenex to the pocket of her house dress.

"Sure were," Mama agreed.

"Lots'a bats too."

"Really?" Mama glanced out the window again, as if she might see one flitting by.

"You didn't see 'em? I must'a seen a dozen from my back porch last night."

Mazy looked toward the curtained-off bedroom. "Do you think Aunt Lavonne'll be alright?" she asked her mama.

"Can't say, Pumpkin. She pretty bad off right now. Why don't you look in on her?"

Mazy pulled at a braid as she always did when she was

asked to do something she dreaded. "She sleepin'. I don't wanna wake her."

Mama smiled as if she approved of Mazy's consideration, but her voice was firm. "Go on, maybe she'd like a sip of water. Jus' tiptoe in and see if she awake."

Mazy, who knew better than to argue with Mama, got up and—avoiding the spot on the floor where Uncle Reginald had died and where she could still see a little of the blood stain, though she and Mama had scrubbed the pine boards with Granny Apple's lye soap and then with vinegar— approached the larger of the house's two bedrooms. The vinegar smell was strong as she pushed through the curtain.

The window curtains were drawn, but there was enough light for her to see the dim form lying under the patchwork quilt.

"She was sittin' in a pool of Reginald's blood, rockin' an' starin' at the wall," she'd overheard their neighbor, Mr. Franklyn, tell Pa.

Mazy shivered. She stepped closer. Aunt Lavonne lay so still that, for a thudding moment, Mazy was seized with panic that she had passed away. Holding her own breath, she leaned close hoping to discern some sign of life.

Aunt Lavonne's eyelids flew open. She bolted upright and her scream cut the air like a carving knife and sent Mazy howling from the room.

ALL DAY MAUVIS FLOWERS TRIED TO CLOSE HER MIND to the unease that had grown stronger and more pervasive since she wrought the spell. The omens augured catastrophe.

For the second day straight, her morning glories had refused to open.

Then there were the strange, almost colorless petals on the marigolds she planted between her tomato plants to keep the bugs off.

Her rain barrel—which held her drinking water—she'd discovered full of tadpoles, though she kept the barrel covered with a cedar lid and couldn't imagine how frogs could have gotten in.

And the worms!

In her tomatoes, in spite of the marigolds. And in her spinach and collards. And mites in her herb garden—all over the undersides of the leaves.

And to top it all off, when she'd come back into the house after giving up on her garden, she'd found six big fat garden slugs in her kitchen, leaving their glistening slime trail on her walls and cabinet doors and floor. Six! Normally, they never came in unless there was a heavy rain, and then no more than an occasional one.

"'Lo, Miz Flowers!'"

The voice, though familiar, startled her. She looked up from her porch chair and the apronful of peas she was shelling and saw Rupert Clemmons coming around the side of the house with his long cane pole over his shoulder, hook, line, sinker, and float wound about the bamboo. He was smiling as he generally did when he'd been fishing in the swamp.

"'Lo, Rupert. How was fishing?" she asked even though

she could see, hanging by a cord from his left hand, a half-dozen fair-sized catfish glistening wetly in the late afternoon light.

"Fine, Miz Flowers. Jes fine." And he held up his catch for her to see. "Sure seen a lotta frogs though," he added, laying his catch by her petunia bed. Leaning his pole against the porch rail, he stooped and pulled two catfish off the stout waxed cord.

"For you, Miz Flowers," he said and held the fish up by the gills for her admiration. The fish were still breathing, gasping, mouths and gills opening and closing spasmodically, whiskers writhing like slow worms.

"Yum, yum!" She smiled despite her worries. "I'm gonna have me fried catfish for supper!"

"Yes, ma'am. Would you like me to set 'em in the kitchen?"

"That'd be kind of you, Rupert. Put 'em in the dishpan by the back door. Oh, and Rupert," she added as he was going in the door. "There's a jar of ginger tea on the table. Help yourself."

Rupert was a good man, one of the very few she shared words with. Most of them weren't worth a hog's fart. Twelve, thirteen years ago she had snatched Rupert from the jaws of death. He'd had a fever that looked like it was going to burn him up. Dr. Campbell, Farnsworth's Black doctor, had given up on him, said he was going to die. Rupert's wife, Nelly, had come to her and begged her to save her man. Mauvis had Rupert's oldest boy catch a bullfrog and she'd tied the bloated thing to the sole of his foot with a sock. Come morning, the frog was dead and Rupert's fever had broke.

Ever since, Rupert brought her fish when he'd had a good

catch and strawberries in the spring and watermelon in the summer. He had patched her roof when it was leaking last year. Only charged her a jar of her persimmon preserves and a jar of her honey.

The screen door opened and Rupert came out, glass in hand. He sat in the second of the cane porch chairs, the one that didn't rock.

"How's the family, Rupert?" she asked as she shelled peas.

"Well, Ellie's got a tetch of the sore throat." He squeezed his own prominent Adam's apple to demonstrate.

"She gargling with honey and lemon, like I told her ma?"

"Yes ma'am. Deed she do."

"And it wouldn't hurt for her to have two, three cups of chamomile tea a day for a couple days. I'll fetch you some soon as I finish these peas."

"Don't bother, Miz Flowers. Nelly's already givin' her the tea. When it comes to nursin', you taught Nelly real good."

Mauvis accepted the compliment with a smile, though most of the remedies she advised to the women who came to her were the same ones their grandmothers had taught them. It was just that, as a root doctor, she had achieved among her neighbors a certain status as a medical authority. In fact, Dr. Campbell had long complained that she stole his patients and that he would have her investigated, though he never had.

Leastways, she didn't play God and try to cure the incurable. Rupert's fever—that had been curable; Dr. Campbell just hadn't known how to root it out of him. But no teas or pills in the world was going to cure a man or a woman eaten up with the cancer.

Ah, but you have played God, haven't you?

"...haven't you?"

"What?" She tried to conceal her startlement.

"I said, 'You got your hands full with this place, haven't you?'"

"Yes." She thought of the slime trails she'd had to scrub off the walls and the worms she'd squashed with her fingers before she'd given up.

"Well..." Rupert slapped his knee and gave himself a boost up. Carefully, he set his empty glass on the porch rail. "I guess I best be gettin' home. Nelly'll be wonderin' some gator got me. Thanky for the tea."

"Thank you for the fish, Rupert. You say hello to Nelly for me."

"I'll do that."

"And send your youngest round next week an' I'll have some mint tea for Nelly to give her strength during the hot weather."

"I'll do that." Rupert paused by the top of the steps, his hand on the whitewashed post. "By the way... I don't mean to be vexin' you, but I know how you all alone here an'...there's been some trouble."

Suddenly, Mauvis felt hot, the way she had when she was going through the change. She didn't really want to hear what Rupert was about to tell her.

"What kind of trouble?"

"Well," Rupert scratched his ear. "I only brung it up because I was thinkin' maybe you should keep your doors and windows locked." She waited and he went on. "Neighbor of mine—good man—name of Reginald Little—" An abyss opened at Mauvis' feet. "—was murdered last night. Everybody's real upset."

"Murdered?" She recalled her coldness to the man,

making him wait on the porch, dismissing him when she saw he was no danger. She had felt the mother's grief but not the father's.

Rupert was nodding. "Yep, right in his own home. And his wife—"

Mauvis jerked forward, nearly upsetting the pan at her feet. "She killed too?"

"No, but I hear tell she's jes starin' an' mutterin' somethin' 'bout the devil."

"Lord a mercy." Mauvis shook her head, clasped her trembling hands in her lap.

"There was a white boy killed last night too. Killed same way."

"How's that?" Looking into Rupert's eyes, she could tell it had been pretty ugly.

Rupert sadly shook his head. "Some crazy person cut their hearts out," he said.

. . .cut their hearts out.

As if a stick of dynamite had exploded in her face, the world went white, and out of the roaring silence rushed a torrent of images.

1924

The embers had died, ashes cold and grey on the scorched brick. Mauvis had let the fire die the night before last and hadn't tried to rekindle it.

She was afraid of what she might see in the embers.

She knew Celia was dead, but as long as she didn't look, she could hope.

All during the endless, despairing night while she stumbled around in the woods and swamp and the next day while the searchers joined her, she had refused to build the fire, knowing she would be unprepared.

For she *knew*—knew beyond a doubt.

The night before last—Thursday evening—when Celia had taken so long returning from Mr. Jacob's grocery store, she'd experienced a horrible feeling—like being slapped in the face and sick on the stomach at the same time. She'd bolted out the door and half ran, half stumbled all the way to the store.

Mr. Jacob must've thought she looked like a crazy woman, bursting into his store out of breath. When he'd figured out she wanted to know if he'd seen Celia, he'd looked up at the big Dr Pepper clock on the wall above the cigarettes, and squinting through his thick, gold-framed spectacles, informed her that Celia had been in but she'd left with five pounds of flour and a box of baking soda over an hour ago. Thanking him, she'd lit out again and spent the night searching and praying, stumbling around in the woods and the edge of the swamp after checking the drainage ditches on both sides of the road and going home to see if maybe, just maybe, Celia was home wondering where her mama had gotten off to.

She hadn't been.

Today, after hours of walking and calling "Celia! Celia!" until she was hoarse, she had finally abandoned the search and gone home, knowing it would take hours to build a good bed of embers. She wanted to be ready by nightfall—when the seeing was clearest. She swept out the hearth, reciting the proper words and sweetening the stone with a sprig of mint before putting on the first cedar log.

The sun set, the stars came out, and still she added wood until the heat in the cabin was stifling and the bed of smoldering red embers grew deep. The inferno threw long shadows behind every object. And now, staring into the glowing pile, she compelled her breathing to slow, her thundering heart to calm. With the charred, fire-tempered end of her grandmother's staff, she poked the embers. Orange lights flared bright within. Sparks flashed up the chimney.

And she saw.

Celia's face, spattered with mud and dried blood; her fogged-over eyes wide and staring and flecked with dirt. A dark stain marked the gaping cavity in her naked chest.

Her heart was missing!

Gasping for breath and clutching a hand to her throat, Mauvis rose and stumbled backwards away from the fire, knocking over her chair. Fighting the tears that threatened to blind her, she resumed her seat and stirred the embers. This time, she sought not to gaze on the present but into the past. She had to know *how* and *why*. Staring into the slithering heat patterns, her jaw grew slack, lips barely mumbling the ancient conjuring words.

Then she was looking up through her baby's eyes at a tall, darkly handsome man who towered above her. The way the man looked at her was blood-chilling. She felt her daughter's terror.

She watched it all, unblinking, transfixed with horror as the man raped and strangled her daughter. Her vision blurred with tears and still she stared.

Then, when she thought it was over, there was more

violence. The deep incision across Celia's chest; the strong black fingers working in between the ribs and pulling them apart; the sickening *snap* of splintering bone; the heart exposed, no longer beating.

When a hand and a knife slid into the cavity to complete the job, her scream left a jagged tear across the night.

THIRTEEN

L uther was pulling the keys out of the ignition when he heard Billy Bob's scream. He assumed it was Billy, though it sounded like a girl.

He had spent the evening at the Red Rooster. He didn't spend much time there anymore—bad for his image with the Ladies Auxiliary and the businessmen—but he liked to drop by once in a while and have a few beers with his hunting buddies. On your average weeknight, you'd probably find Elwood Langsmith and his brother Pete—big men who cut timber—Artie Mulholland, Craig Potts, Ed Tingle, Ralph Bowlard—all farmers—Hunt Griffith, who had made a living wrestling alligator until he lost half a hand. Course, his deputy, Hank, would usually show up. Dewey McFarland, together with his oldest boy, Albert, who wasn't much younger than Luther, were occasionally in attendance; Dewey's shine put the Red Rooster's liquor selection to shame.

Tonight, the whole crew had shown up. Luther figured

they would after last night's events. Probably every man, woman, and politician in Farnsworth or in Caledonia— maybe in the entire county—knew about the murders and were speculating to high heaven about what kind of maniac would kill a person and then cut his heart out, and what in the world would the maniac use the hearts for.

Most of the men present had family and they wanted to know what he was doing to protect them (never mind that their families would be better protected if the menfolk stayed home instead of going out to drink and speculate).

"Is it true, Luther, that the killer disappeared into the swamp?" Roy Hanson asked. Roy had been in Korea too. Marines. Luther had tried to get him to sign on as deputy before he'd hired TJ, but Roy's wife didn't hold with guns, even gave Roy a hard time about killing deer. "Dewey says the killer rubbed some kind of weed on him that confused his dogs." Everybody knew that Dewey could be counted on to stretch the truth.

At a corner table, Dewey scowled sagaciously. Luther was careful not to offend the old man. "Yeah, whoever it is is pretty slick. Takes cunning to fool Dewey's hounds." Dewey nodded, as if agreeing with some profound bit of Biblical wisdom.

The next thing he knew, somebody put a beer in his hand and the questions had begun in earnest.

Luther drew his revolver as he took the porch steps two at a time and flung open the front door.

Stupid kid, he thought, *he didn't even lock up*. Although the boy was usually pretty good about carrying out the orders he gave him.

Unless somebody else had opened it...

His neck hairs prickled like porcupine quills as he scanned the floor for sand. Billy had stopped screaming. Feeling in the air, Luther pulled the cord; light flooded the hall. He approached Billy's door, noting with relief that he didn't hear the grating of sand beneath his shoes.

Switching on Billy's light, he saw that his son was alone. The boy was sitting up, blinking. He looked disoriented and scared, as if he'd had a nightmare. Luther frowned, feeling the injustice of being cursed with a weak-willed son. If Billy Bob fell apart, how, for Christ's sake, was the boy going to keep his cronies in line?

"You don't look too good, Son," he observed. "Maybe you ain't cut out for this kind of work."

"What kind of work is that?"

Luther grinned, shrugged. "Tough guy stuff."

"'TOUGH GUY STUFF,'" BILLY BOB MIMICKED AND immediately regretted sassing Pa. But he was feeling bitter and jealous that Pa could joke when his own insides were ravaged by guilt and terror? And the dream... He couldn't shake the sensation of quicksand surrounding him, slithering over his body, sucking him under.

"You mockin' me Boy?" Pa said. The liquored gleam in his eye had turned nasty.

"No, sir. It's just that I don't feel well."

Standing beside the bed, Pa folded his big arms across his chest. "You don't feel well because your spine's comin' unglued. You'd be amazed how short you'd be without a spine. Not exactly the type of person people look up to." Pa's small blue eyes glittered dangerously behind narrowed lids. "That boy's dead, Son," he hissed through clenched teeth. Billy smelled the beer on Pa's breath. "And you're alive. So why the fuck're you screamin' like some goddamned woman with a broom up her ass?"

Billy shrank before his pa's anger.

"Don't cringe, Boy. I ain't raised no damned jellyfish!" Pa hauled him out of bed by his pajama top so fast Billy got a rush of giddiness in his stomach like he did when he closed his eyes on the swings. He felt like a stuffed toy in Pa's hand. His pajama top ripped up the back and he collapsed to his knees. "Get off your knees, Boy!" Pa—his big fist twisting the cotton fabric at Billy's throat—yanked him to his feet.

Billy Bob gasped for air, his fat cheeks and wide lips working like a dying fish. It was going to happen. Now! The thing he dreaded most in the world: Pa was going to punch his teeth out the back of his head! He scrunched his eyes closed and turned his face so Pa would hit him on the side of the head instead of in his nose or mouth.

But Pa grunted disgust and released him. Billy collapsed. "Don't worry, I'm not gonna hit you. You might bleed all over my uniform. But if you don't get up and get back in bed, I'm gonna kick the tar out of you. Now scoot!"

Billy scooted. His pajama bottoms bunched up around his knees when he shoved his legs under the sheet. Pa pulled the light cord. Backlighted by the hall, his face in shadow, his broad shoulders nearly filling up the door, Pa jabbed a blunt finger at him. "I'm warnin' you, Son—you get some sleep. You look like hell, an' I don't want nobody askin' you what's wrong. I ain't raisin' no wimp! You're involved in a murder an' in the highly illegal disposal of a body. Childhood's over for you. I want you grown up by mornin'. You hear me, Billy Bob?"

"Yes." Billy's reply was a choked whisper.

"'Yes,' what?"

"Yes, sir, I hear you."

"Fine. And don't forget—lest you think it was all a dream —there's a body out there in that quicksand hole. And it's probably lonely; so, 'less you want to join it, I suggest you unpucker your butt an' quit mopin'. Understand me?"

"Yes, sir."

Pa closed the door and Billy listened to the Sheriff making his way to the bathroom. Lying on his back in the shallow depression he had worn into the mattress, he stretched his spine to its fullest. Despite being humiliated and threatened with death, Billy was glad his old man was home. Perhaps now the nightmares would leave him alone. Tomorrow, he'd get the others together and take them hiking so he could keep an eye on them. Take Mauser along to remind them how big his teeth are. Pa would be proud of him yet. He had no intention of ending up in the quicksand hole!

But as he basked in the imagined sunshine of his father's praise, he remembered Lance was dead and wondered who would be missing a heart come morning.

FOURTEEN

The little girl's name is Nancy. She is six and she is deep asleep.

Suddenly, Nancy sees a terrifying face, all white skull and dripping blood. Her parents do not tell her Bloody Bones stories, but she knows them well. Missy Dooley's brother Tom is always scaring her and Diane, another girlfriend from their first-grade class, when they sleep over at Missy's. She recognizes the face at once, but sensing it is a dream, she doesn't scream.

Nor does she wake when the window latch jerks itself open. Or as the window slides silently up. She sleeps the sleep of a child exhausted from hard play.

As the dark shape slips over the sill.

HE WAS BOCOR.

In Haiti, his uncle—with whom he had lived and who was houngan for the community in the squalid suburb of Port au Prince—had guided him through the initiation ceremony that lasted nine days during which he lay on his belly, naked and fasting on the ground under the feather and snakeskin shawl that was the regalia of his uncle's power and with his face in a dry hole in the earth except to sip from a water jar once in a while. From the third day on, he hallucinated and had many visions.

As houngan, his uncle served the spiritual needs of the community, as well as providing the continuity, the seasonal rhythm, of tradition. Consulting and pacifying the ancestral dead, dealing with the loa, and honoring the deities were his uncle's domain, and his uncle had instructed him expecting he would prepare himself for the same calling. But he had understood at an early age that there was more money in selling aphrodisiacs and the left-handed gris-gris that helped men ruin or drive off their rivals in love and business than in tending the hounfor.

He murdered his uncle for the shawl of snakeskins and feathers and fled to Jamaica. Among the cluttered tenements and narrow flyblown alleys of Kingston he set up shop, plying a brisk trade in fetishes and counter spells. With his shawl and his hard, handsome face, he cut an imposing figure.

By day, his clientele grew; by night, he developed an inhuman appetite.

His first victim was an eleven-year-old girl, a red-haired beauty, tall for her age, her legs long, her breasts just beginning to swell against her blouse. He had strangled her when he finished with her.

After that, adult women could no longer satisfy him. When he was with one, his fantasies would turn to visions of the girl, her face purpling under his thumbs as he came, spasming, jerking, grimacing, *squeezing*...until he was spent and the girl was a broken doll.

Giving in to his lusts, letting them rear and plunge and kill, he sought the young, the vulnerable, and satiated himself.

Eventually, he was suspected, but he foresaw his arrest through his communion with L'inglesou, the powerful mystery whose attribute is a dagger plunged into a heart, the image drawn in blood and sprinkled with blood to give the veve a soul, and he himself partook of the blood to open the line of communication. With the money he made in Jamaica, he bought passage on a midnight steamer and fled to Miami, to Little Havana where his practices had more in common with the widespread Santeria than with the Catholic Church. By now, not wanting to appear conspicuous in case the law pursued him to the United States, he had disposed of his uncle's shawl, having learned that it is not the trappings that bestows power on the bocor but knowing the words and the conditions of power.

And blood.

Much blood.

He blood-sucked Miami for a while then moved on, dropping his Creole accent as fast as he could absorb the local dialect as he traveled rural Florida and Georgia working on the sawmill gang, the road gang, the turpentine gang, or passing himself off as a sharecropper or a preacher. Oh, how the natives loved a Bible-thumping preacher. The Bible is the great conjure book and he knew it well. He knew the secret verse in the Book of Ezekiel which, if read with the right attitude and under the right conditions, will stop bleeding; knew the lives and the ceremonies of the Old Testament bocors: Solomon and Moses, who were the greatest bocors until the birth of Christ; knew which verses could be spoken backwards over a handful of goofer dust on a certain night to raise the dead.

But now his body—his hard, handsome body that had drawn women and men to him, with its persuasive visage that had silenced children into submissiveness—was gone, rotted into bones at the bottom of a sink hole, and his soul was condemned to a twilight existence in a piece of animated, impotent meat.

He burned and his fist tightened on the wooden haft of the butcher knife. Fantasies of hacking, garroting, slow bleeding, strangling, poisoning—feverish images of blood and a pleading, horrorstruck face—the face of his undoer—spurred him on.

His mind settled on the Death by a Thousand Cuts, an infamous tool of the Inquisition and still hard to outdo five centuries later; and he paused, his dead feet planted in the dew-soaked grass, his fists clenched, and let his thoughts take him down a roaring red river of vengeance.

In his fantasy, the witch was bound hand and foot and lay naked under the starlight in the wet grass. Not old as she must be now, but as he remembered her, tall and handsome, square-shouldered and high-titted, the way he liked them. Her creamy mocha-colored skin glistened with fear-sweat. In his fantasy, he cut out her tongue to keep her screams from being heard a mile away, and in the fantasy, he sliced her a thousand times, small incisions with a piece of glass, avoiding major arteries but collectively fatal.

The first slice, he decided, would be her eye. He'd leave the other till the end, so she could see what was happening to her.

Not tonight. Tonight, he had other cats to skin.

But soon, he thought as he quickened his step.

Soon.

THE THICK WHITE PLATE SAILING ACROSS THE kitchen, cleaving the air like a flying saucer; his father throwing his arm up to keep it from hitting him in the face; the plate breaking on his father's arm; the bright red splash of blood that followed the pieces to the floor; the look on his father's face as he gaped at the long ragged tear in his forearm; the roar in his head that might have been his parents shouting or might have been the noise of his tumbling thoughts; Pa fishing for his car keys as he ran to the door, a dish towel wrapped around his arm; Ma stomping over, still cursing, and slamming the door—the day's events, recorded as if by movie camera, played back. Over and over, Whitey dreamed the bright splash of blood and his father's shocked expression. The tense silence that followed after the sound of Pa's pickup faded down the road; his ma chain-smoking three cigarettes, then getting up and turning on the radio and going about cleaning up the shattered plate as if nothing had happened; Pa returning hours later with Deputy Hank, who told Ma she could go to jail for cutting somebody like that—these, too, his mind reviewed; but the blood and his father's face were prominent.

Now, as if his mind tired of the repetition of the white plate and the bright blood, he saw his parents playing Tug-of-War with him, pulling him by his arms in opposite directions till he felt as if he would split in half like Rumpelstiltskin. Not an illustration from yesterday, but one in which he'd been the central actor more times than he could remember since he was a toddler.

In his dream state he was aware that he was at Jimmy's house; and knowing that he was in Jimmy's room with Jimmy sleeping right beside him and that his parents were half a mile away, he felt better. Since Jimmy had befriended him, he no longer accepted violence as the normal way of life.

A voice suddenly spoke through the ugly roar in his head. A low, scary voice that chilled his veins. *I Bloody Bones, an' I comin' to get you.*

JIMMY WAS A LIGHT SLEEPER; AND, THOUGH HIS window slid open as silently as a snake slithering over smooth stone, the stealthy grating woke him. In time to see the black shape standing next to the bed on Whitey's side; in time to see by the starlight the knife upraised over Whitey's face.

"*NOOO!*" Jimmy screamed. Grabbing Whitey and rolling, he hurled them both onto the floor on his side of the bed. The blade buried itself with a *whoomph* in Whitey's pillow.

Untangling his legs from Whitey's, Jimmy scrambled to his feet and pulled the overhead cord. Light flooded the room, revealed the creature which hopped onto the bed brandishing the long butcher knife.

Jimmy didn't believe in ghosts any more than he believed in witches or Bloody Bones or the Tooth Fairy or the twenty-foot alligator that was said to live in the swamp. Nor did he believe the stories about people seeing old Hannah Quince standing stark naked and headless on her porch some mornings about five-thirty a.m.—the hour she was murdered fifty years ago. These fears he had sincerely believed behind him, tucked away in a drawer along with his baby shoes and rattle. But the red-eyed, knife-wielding thing glaring at him, dripping blood and wet sand as it sprang, was no scare tale.

Jimmy ducked as the blade whistled toward his throat. "You!" was all he could say as his body thrummed with shock.

Lamar's corpse landed between him and Whitey. Though Whitey's mouth and eyes were perfect O's of horror, all that issued from his throat was a thin whine of escaping air. Lamar turned toward Whitey. Jimmy grabbed the wooden rung-back chair by the bed and slammed it into the ghost as hard as he could. Surprisingly, since he'd half expected the chair to go right through it, the apparition was knocked to the floor.

"Come on!" Jimmy grabbed Whitey's hand, yanked him to his feet, and ran for the door. He glanced back as he shoved his pal ahead of him. He hoped Granny didn't wake; she was too old to run. The ghost was on its feet, charging.

"*It's stuck!*" Whitey screamed at the top of his lungs. "*The door won't open!*"

GRANNY DOBBINS WOKE. SHE DIDN'T PAUSE TO wonder if the noise in the next room was part of a dream because Jimmy was yelling, "Come on!"

"Oh, Lord!" she said, climbing out of bed and hurrying barefoot into the hall.

Jimmy's door was rattling and Whitey was screaming, *"It's stuck! The door won't open!"*

She pulled the light cord, and her heart lurched like a bad transmission when something hit the door on the other side and several inches of butcher knife slammed through a panel.

"LOOK OUT!" JIMMY SCREAMED AND HURLED WHITEY aside as the blade slammed through the door.

"Jimmy!" Granny yelled on the other side.

"Stay away, Granny!" Jimmy yelled back.

Growling like an animal, Lamar wrenched the knife free and spun, lashing out as he turned. Jimmy raised his hands to ward off the blow. The blade, razor sharp, slid across his left wrist, severing veins. Jimmy stared in shock at the spurting crimson. The vision was too dreamlike to be real.

"Out the window!" he shouted to Whitey as he backed away, knowing deep down, no matter how his mind tried to deceive him, he'd just been badly cut and Granny's screams, the knife-wielding ghost, the blood flowing through his fingers as he tried to hold the wound together were all too real.

The ghost smiled at him. Its eyes blazed like a demon's. In the uncompromising light of the hundred-watt bulb, Jimmy saw clearly the ragged, puffed up wounds in the child's throat and belly, the coil of dripping gut. The rotten meat smell was eye-watering.

Wary of the blade pointed at his stomach, near panicking with the knowledge that his life was ebbing and that if he didn't get to a doctor soon he was a goner, Jimmy pleaded with the apparition. "I understand your wanting to get even. I tried to stop it. Honest!"

There were tears in Jimmy's eyes, not of fear, but of compassion for the innocent before him, this poor kid who'd been flying his kite and minding his own business.

Ghosts of murdered folks can't rest until the murderer's caught! Hadn't he heard something like that somewhere?

Granny rattled the door. "Open up, Jimmy, open up! Oh God oh God!"

"I'll tell the newspaper what happened, then everybody will know and you can rest in peace. Okay?"

As if in answer, the ghost opened its mouth and kept opening it till it looked as if it would scream at him. From the black maw shot a stream of quicksand that arced between them and struck Jimmy in the eyes, blinding him. The vomit-like scent gagged him as the sand ran down his chest, plastering his pajamas to his body.

"Run!" he screamed over his shoulder.

"Jimmy!" Whitey howled, straddling the windowsill,

ready to bolt, but unwilling to desert his friend. Tears stung his eyes as Jimmy turned blindly toward the ghost and the long, keen edge slid across his throat, sinking effortlessly through the flesh.

THE DARK MAN WHOOPED, HIS VOICE LOUDER NOW that he had disgorged some of the sand in his lungs. The old woman was hammering at the door, which he willed firmly shut. The other boy, Whitey, was out the window and running barefoot around the side of the house heading for the road. The Dark Man felt the child's heart pounding, like a kid banging a stick against a fifty-gallon drum, felt the damp night air ripping in and out of his lungs, the fear burning like acid in his veins.

The Dark Man glanced at the dead boy on the floor, at the rattling door; then, with the old woman's cries fading behind him, he was out the window and racing after Whitey.

Rounding the corner of the house, he saw the child turn out of the graveled driveway into the road. The Dark Man accelerated, his new feet pattering over the wet grass that he could not feel and then kicking up gravel that caused no pain. The night was clear and the stars shone wanly on the narrow two-lane road.

The boy was quick, but the Dark Man had the excitement of a fresh kill and the promise of another to spur his heels. Now he was on the road, closing in, dead feet pattering on the blacktop. The boy glanced back and yelped, then leaned forward and sped up. The Dark Man cursed; the boy was faster than he'd expected. But he heard and felt the wild thumping of the boy's heart, the ragged tearing of wind in and out of his lungs, the roaring of blood in his veins. His own heart was dead, his lungs clotted with quicksand, his veins emptied. The boy would tire; he would not. He smiled, quicksand oozing from his grey lips, and tightened his grip on the knife.

Trees swept by in the starlight, black sentinels lining a grey road, and now a house set back from the street, dark as the trees, silent. Then more trees and another house and a field beyond that. The gap closed.

And now the boy was only a few yards ahead, and though the corpse's ears were filled with quicksand, the Dark Man could hear the boy's hitching breath, the faint whine that escaped when he exhaled. The Dark Man readied himself for the plunge of the knife that would slam the boy off his feet— when, suddenly, as he had the morning before, he felt the tug of the quicksand hole and his rebellious feet carried him off the road and onto a field, racing toward the woods. Though the eastern horizon was still black, forest and field merging with sky, he felt the weight of the approaching sun. It was a boulder bigger than a mountain rolling ponderously toward him; any moment now, it would bound over the horizon and crush him.

If it caught him outside the quicksand hole.

FIFTEEN

"He said his name was Bloody Bones."
"But you just said it was Lamar Little you saw."
"Yes, but—"
"You said he chased you."
"Yes."
"And then, all of a sudden, he's runnin' across a field."
"Yes."
"Why'd he let you go?"
"I don't know."
"Why'd he kill Jimmy Dobbins?"
"I don't know."
"How do you know it was Lamar Little?"
"Because he looked like him, and..."
"Yes?"
"He was dead."
Luther put his conversation with Eugene "Whitey"

Creedy out of his thoughts as he slammed into the control room snapping orders on his way to his office.

"Connie," he said to the plump dyed-blond woman surrounded by a typewriter, a dispatch radio, and a telephone, "get Dewey McFarland on the horn. Tell him to meet me at the Dobbins' place. He knows Frank Dobbins. Tell him to bring his boy Jeb and three or four of his best hounds. And tell him not the three he brung yesterday."

"Right."

"Mornin', Lyle."

The balding jailkeeper, who had retired four years ago and returned to work one morning three weeks later complaining he could take only so much fishing, grunted, "Mornin'," around the cigarette that dangled from a corner of his mouth.

"TJ, in my office."

TJ, sitting at a desk with a newspaper open before him, started to speak but Connie beat him to it.

"Oh, Luther?"

"Yeah?" Luther stopped with one foot in his office.

Mayor Hanley said for you to call him soon as you come in."

"Jesus!" Last thing he needed right now was to spend an hour repeating everything he'd learned from his interview with the Creedy kid and his subsequent visit to the Wenton place, responding to a report of a missing six-year-old girl. Hanley, the fat hand-shaking bastard, would probably choke on his cigar if he told him about the bloody child-sized foot-prints found at the murder scenes and the quicksand found on Nancy Wenton's windowsill. "If he calls back, tell him I'll call him soon as I get in."

"Right."

Dropping his bulk into his desk chair, Luther turned to the homicides with the tireless energy of a dog chewing a bone.

Because he looked like him...

A cousin then? He scratched the word on his desk calendar. Someone who bore a strong resemblance to Lamar Little at any rate. Someone about the same age and size. If Creedy had actually seen what he said he'd seen, which he doubted. Kid was so shit-scared and so full of guilt, he'd probably hallucinated. He'd have to keep an eye on that boy. He was a loose cannon that might very well cost him his reelection and land him in jail.

Someone knocked his door. "Come in."

TJ entered carrying a stack of yellowed newspapers and dog-eared ledgers. The green covers of the latter were warped and mildewed. TJ started to place the ledgers and newspapers on the corner of Luther's desk.

"Don't you lay that crap on my desk, Boy. I ain't the prettiest thing in Farnsworth, but do you want to see me really ugly?"

TJ shook his head, steadying the precarious mound. "No, wouldn't want to rile you, Boss. Surely wouldn't want to do that."

TJ was being sarcastic, but there was no bitterness in it and Luther preferred sarcasm to a yes man any day. Sarcasm took a little brains. "That the stuff I asked you to get together for me yesterday?"

"Yep."

"Well," Luther leaned back and folded his hands on his washboard gut, "here's what I want you to do with it, TJ."

TJ's smile faded. "I'm not going to like this, but go ahead."

"Well, thank you, Thomas Jefferson. Me 'n' Hank's goin' hunting. You're gonna watch the store. Connie'll handle the phones, but the press, maybe even some curious citizens, might come in here demanding to know what's goin' on. All you say is Sheriff Wilcox is searching for the missing girl and you'll have to wait till he gets back if you have any further questions. You don't know nothin' more'n they do. And don't speculate.

"Now, when you ain't doin' kiss ass work I want you to go through those." He nodded at the journals and newspapers. "Boil it down for me. I want an account of every body found with a missin' heart. I want addresses, witnesses or family of victims who're still alive. Lyle can help you with that; he knows everybody in Farnsworth. Get yourself some coffee and get to work before the press gets here."

The intercom buzzed as the door closed behind TJ.

"Yes?"

"Mayor's on the line."

"You tell the mayor—"

"He saw your car out front, Luther."

"Well, tell him to look again! But leave him on hold for a minute, will ya?" Luther hung up, grabbed his hat, and, hauling his keys from his pocket, hurried out of the office.

"YOU'RE GONNA GET THE 'LECTRIC CHAIR FOR SURE," Skeeter threatened as he paced up and down in front of them on the sunlit path beside the creek.

"But I ain't done nothin'!" Whitey whined and turned to Steven for support.

Steven, sitting beside Whitey on the moss-grown log, had listened to the boy's tale—told through sobs which earned him derision from Skeeter. His story conjured frightening visions in Steven's imagination.

Jimmy dead! He and Jimmy had gone to kindergarten together. His throat cut! And, according to Whitey, by the ghost of Lamar Little calling himself Bloody Bones (though that last part was probably a dream). Skeeter wasn't buying any of it, but Steven knew Whitey was too honest to make up such a fib.

Billy Bob, who sat on a rock staring gloomily at the ground between his feet, was off on another planet. If Steven didn't know him better, he'd have said Billy was suffering from a case of the guilts.

When Billy Bob called him that morning and told him to meet him by the creek, he hadn't mentioned Jimmy. When Steven arrived, Billy Bob and Mauser had been waiting. Presently, Skeeter and Whitey came along, and soon as Steven saw Whitey's face, he knew something was bad wrong. And before he could yell, "Where's Jimmy?" Skeeter said, "Hey, did you hear? Dobbins is dead!"

"'But I ain't done nothin'!'" Skeeter mimicked Whitey. He stopped before the younger boy and leaned over him, his long neck thrust forward like a buzzard's. "Sure, Bloody Bones killed Jimmy Dobbins! Or was it a ghost? You ain't too clear on that, are you, Creedy?"

"I—"

"Judge don't believe in Bloody Bones or in ghosts. You were the only one in the room with him. Tell us the truth—

you cut Jimmy, then ran away and hid the knife." Whitey shook his head. "Then you came back and told the Sheriff some cockamamie story you made up. Ain't that right? Ain't it?" He poked Whitey in his scrawny chest. "You gonna burn, you freak! B-u-r-n, burn!" He tapped out the words on top of Whitey's head with a bony index finger.

"Aw, leave him alone, Skeeter," Steven said, not wanting to attract Skeeter's attention, but fed up with his prattling.

Sure enough, Skeeter turned on him, glaring and thrusting a finger, his grin gone as suddenly as his face had reddened. "You stay outta this, Blankenship!"

"Can't you see Whitey's in shock?" Steven said, holding Skeeter's gaze though his stomach fluttered. "He should be seeing a doctor!"

"Do you see anybody here who gives a fart, Four Eyes?" Skeeter shouted in his face. Steven closed his eyes against the fine spray of spittle.

"Four eyes? But I don't wear glasses."

"You will—after I punch out both your eyes!" Skeeter laughed at his cleverness.

Steven was careful not to grin, relieved that Skeeter had decided to make him the butt of his joke rather than pulverize him. *Sticks and stones*, Steven thought.

But Mauser was on his feet, eyeing Skeeter and Steven and growling low and ominous. Steven froze.

"Mauser, *sit!*" Billy Bob yelled and yanked the leash. It was the first he'd spoken in twenty minutes, and the act of looking up and yelling had brought some of his color back. To everyone's relief, Mauser sat; though, to Steven's mind, with his tongue hanging out panting from the summer heat, the Doberman seemed to regard him hungrily.

"Skeeter," Billy Bob said, "why don't you sit down and shut your trap?"

"Aw, I ain't botherin' Mauser," Skeeter sulked, but he stayed quiet, and for a minute or two, they could hear the creek flowing by the grassy bank.

In that quiet moment, Steven thought how he and Whitey and Billy Bob and Skeeter shared a bond that, in a way, was as close as family; never mind how different they were and how much some of them disliked each other. They shared the same fate—they were each marked for the slaughter.

That reminded him of what his uncle had once told him about how cowboys put a special brand on cattle to be slaughtered.

After chucking a few stones into the creek, Skeeter said to Billy Bob, "Hey, Billy, let's go to the playground and have some fun, huh?"

Billy Bob frowned. "Skeeter, why don't you shut up? Maybe take a dip in the creek?"

Steven half expected Skeeter to turn on Billy Bob. It would be suicide, but Skeeter had a hair-trigger temper. Instead, he smiled, showing his crooked teeth, and said, "Good idea. Here's a dip!" He grabbed Whitey by the wrist, dragged him across the path, and hurled him into the creek.

Whitey went down with a splash. He was up in an instant, sputtering and bellowing as he rushed the bank where Skeeter stood roaring with laughter.

Whitey slipped on the grass and went down again. When he came up, his face red, his almost colorless eyebrows bunched together, he launched himself at his tormentor, bursting from the water as if he'd been sitting on a spring. His fist hurtled toward the bully's jaw.

It happened so fast, Steven didn't catch the individual movements but saw what happened next as a swift blur of action of which he was a part. Skeeter caught Whitey's fist, spun the smaller boy around, and pinned his arm behind his back. Steven was on his feet, leaping, not thinking about the foolishness of what he was doing; and the next thing he knew, he was riding Skeeter piggyback, his legs locked around Skeeter's waist, an arm clamped around his skinny neck.

Suddenly released, Whitey went flying back into the water and Steven and Skeeter tumbled onto the path, Steven on top.

Mauser was growling again, and now he barked and Steven heard Billy Bob yell, "Heel!" and Steven hoped Mauser heeled because he had his hands full.

Slowly, Skeeter muscled Steven over until Steven was looking up into a mask of rage. Steven got in the first punch. It wasn't a conscious decision; he saw Skeeter's rage and landed a blow before he got clobbered. His fist connected with Skeeter's left eye and the bigger boy turned loose. Steven struggled to rise, but Skeeter, madder than a hornet, seized the front of his tee shirt, drew back his fist, and returned the favor. Steven's vision became a kaleidoscope of red and jangling lights; pain exploded like an afterthought.

An arrow of dazzling sunlight pierced his migraine. When his vision returned, he was on the ground and Skeeter was drawing back his fist for another punch. Mauser was barking and Whitey was shouting.

A hand grabbed Skeeter's wrist from behind. It was Billy Bob looking mean and displeased. The muscles in Billy Bob's arm bulged beneath the fat as he pulled Skeeter off Steven with one hand. Mauser growled like a wolf. The black hair bristled on the back of the dog's neck. Steven saw that Billy

Bob had tied the leash to a root. He hoped the leather strap held.

The punched side of his face ached and was starting to swell. Whitey was standing in the shallow water, his tee shirt and cutoffs wet and clinging to his skinny body. Billy Bob had the fore and middle fingers of Skeeter's right hand up in the air bent backwards so that Skeeter followed on tiptoe wherever Billy led.

Billy led Skeeter over to Mauser. Mauser stopped straining at his leash and watched Skeeter as if his master was bringing him a treat.

"Good boy, Mauser," Skeeter said. His face was red, his voice thin with pain, yet he wore a big smile for Mauser. Luckily for Skeeter, the Doberman was already at the end of his leash.

Billy Bob bent Skeeter a little closer. A sinister growl rumbled deep in Mauser's throat.

"Didn't I ask you politely to shut the fuck up?" Billy Bob applied more pressure on Skeeter's fingers, bending him toward the waiting Doberman.

"Cut it out, Billy! You're hurtin' me!"

"How would you like me to throw you on top of Mauser?"

Skeeter tried to twist free, but Billy wrenched the captive fingers and bent the gangling bully another inch closer to the Doberman. Straining at his leash, Mauser barked in Skeeter's face.

"I told you to shut up, didn't I?"

"I'm shushed, ain't I?" Skeeter said.

Billy Bob released his hand. Skeeter jumped away from Mauser and, glaring razor blades at Billy Bob, massaged his sore fingers. Realizing Steven and Whitey were watching him, he stopped massaging and balled his hand into a fist till his knuckles cracked.

"Well, you can just hang out with Blankenship and the albino," he growled at Billy Bob.

"I ain't no albino!" Whitey yelled, coming up onto the bank. "I just got white hair!"

"Albino!"

Mauser was barking again.

Will you shut your big stupid trap, Francis!"

Skeeter stopped dancing. His jack-in-the-box grin melted off his face like candle wax. Whitey giggled. Mauser barked. Skeeter's ears burned red.

"Nuts to you creeps," he said. "I'm goin' home an' read some comic books."

"You ain't got no comics," Billy Bob said.

"Yeah? Well, my brother Mark's got two Bat Man comics and a funny they gave him at the shoe store," Skeeter called over his shoulder as he walked away.

"Bloody Bones is gonna get you!" It was Whitey who shouted, spitting out the words as if they were darts aimed at Skeeter's back.

Skeeter turned. "I ain't scared of no Bloody Bones!" he yelled through his cupped hands.

CLAREMONT JACOB, WHO HAD INHERITED THE STOP & Go groceries on Peabody Road from his father, Ralph Jacob, picked his way over the rotting log, careful not to touch the poison ivy he saw coiled about its bark. The three-lobed leaves glistened oilily in the afternoon sunlight. Twenty-six men had turned out to search for the Wenton girl. Probably be a few cases of poison ivy come tomorrow. Out of habit, he tried to recall if he had a good stock of calamine lotion back at the store.

Personally, Claremont didn't think they'd find the girl alive—not after the two boys and Reginald Little. Of course, those bodies had been left lying where they were killed. The girl was a victim of a kidnapping. Technically, the law might look on the girl's disappearance as unrelated to the murders; but Farnsworth was a small town, and it was too far-fetched that a murder and a kidnapping committed on the same night were unrelated.

The day had heated up to over ninety. The humidity rose the closer he got to the swamp. His hair was plastered to his head under his nylon fishing cap—white with a green-and-black patch featuring a trout jumping out of water. His cotton shirt clung to his back. Every so often about ten yards off to his left, he'd see Henry Barnes in his red-and-black plaid flannel. Claremont couldn't see how the old coot could stand wearing a flannel in this heat. About the same distance on his right was Burt Larkins, who worked for the County Roads Commission. The search seemed hopeless. Spread out as they were and with the many hidey holes the forest offered, they could walk right by and not see her.

Claremont stopped to mop his face. His legs ached. He'd be fifty-six come fall. Not old at all. Not really. But fishing wasn't the most strenuous exercise, and ringing up the cash register surely wasn't turning the pork to beef.

Moving on, he came to a low hill and started to go around

it, but it wasn't very high—actually little more than a rise in the low-lying land—and he figured it'd afford him a good vantage point to survey the ground ahead. He came over the rise and started down the other side. And there, in a cut in the hillside where the Georgia red clay had eroded, lay the body of Nancy Wenton.

Emma and he had been unable to have a child. Emma had always wanted a little girl, and his heart went out to Nancy's parents as he made his way to the body, even though they probably shopped the Piggly Wiggly on Dixie Highway.

The Wenton girl was lying face up, head downhill, one of her little legs crooked under the other like a figure four. She was nude and her eyes were missing, probably pecked out by a jay or crow. The flies boiled off the carcass when he waved his cap over it. The buzzing was like the drone of a single-engine plane.

And then he saw what the flies had been feasting on. Dozens more still lined the crater in the little girl's chest.

SIXTEEN

The pool in the creek had most likely been built by kids since grownups didn't have time for such nonsense. Stones and sticks stacked across the stream formed a wide sandy-bottomed area. A short dam spilled over the makeshift damn. The water was clear, no more than two feet deep in the middle. Several large flat stones around its rim and two in the pool itself made it easy to maneuver about.

Skeeter's first impulse when he came upon the pool, was to destroy the dam— destruction typically being Skeeter's first thought when looking upon another's creation—but then he saw the fish. Five fat yellow perch.

Whoever put the fish here obviously hadn't considered how shallow the creek was, and though the leaves overhead partly shaded the pool, the light-brown sand reflected the sunlight, warming the water, and the fish waited out the heat in the shadows of the rocks. Standing on one of the central rocks, Skeeter exchanged stares with each of the fish in turn. It annoyed him that they failed to display the proper terror and madly seek to bury themselves under the rocks.

Stepping back onto the forest trail, he walked downstream until he found a four-foot length of grey, barkless branch. Splintered at both ends, it could serve as a spear as well as a club. Stick in hand, he returned to the pool

Before happening upon the fish, Skeeter had farted around in the woods, too pissed to go home. He'd probably get into a fight with one of his older brothers and he'd get throttled. Then he'd smack his younger brother and Pa or his older brothers would whup him again. Which might not be so bad; he felt like getting into a ruckus. But he also felt like being alone to think, though with Skeeter thinking wasn't conscious thought but more like roaring red impressions of violence. The only time he applied conscious thought was when some particularly choice bit of devilment seized his imagination. He never wasted concentration on anything as unrewarding as schoolwork.

In pictures, he thought how he might have gotten into it with Billy Bob if Mauser hadn't been there. Billy Bob had been looking and acting as wimpy as Whitey, moping on his rock, not threatening anybody. He imagined punching Billy Bob in the face and seeing him go down, imagined kicking fat boy when he tried to get up. The pictures felt good—a poor substitute for the real thing—but good.

And Blankenship... Skeeter had been surprised how hard he could punch. His eye ached and he was glad to stay in the shade of the trees because the sunlight felt like splinters. But he grinned at the images of what he was going to do to Blankenship next time he ran into him.

Returning to the central rock, Skeeter surveyed his prey. This time, as he noisily smacked the stick against his palm, he thought they regarded him more warily. They seemed to move deeper into the slim shadows of the rocks, their gills and fins working more frantically. "Okay," he said, feeling an electric thrill of anticipation, "which of you guys is first?"

Basking in the godlike stature the club and the fish's vulnerability bestowed upon him, he regarded them each in turn. Somehow, they'd all managed to position themselves so that one eye was pivoted toward him, gills rippling, tails and fins treading water, tiny fish mouths working.

They're afraid! he thought, immensely pleased that fish could feel terror.

He had killed a mouse once. It had gotten into a garbage can and couldn't jump back out. Little thing, couldn't have been more than three inches long. The noise of the creature jumping against the sheer cliff of galvanized steel had attracted him to the trash can by the side of the house; and when the mouse saw him peering over the rim, it had gone into a frenzy of terror, racing round and round and hurling itself against the walls. Breathless with excitement, he had hurried into the house.

He'd returned with his pa's fillet knife, which had a long skinny blade and orange plastic handle. The mouse had been hard to pin down, and once it had attempted to run up his arm, giving him an unpleasant dose of fear. He'd steadied himself, holding the knife point inches off the bottom of the can as the mouse sped round and round. He lunged. The tip of the blade plunged into the mouse's side, pinned it to the bottom. The thing went wild, scrabbling like it was trying to run and its teeth chattering on the knife.

Skeeter recalled the heady, stomach-knotting exhilaration he had felt watching the mouse slump on the knife, no longer protesting, the tremendous beating of its heart, the blood trickling out of its mouth and nostrils, and, finally, the glaze that fogged over the dead eyes and the frozen posture of its teeth and paws.

Feeling that exhilaration now, Skeeter raised the rude club over his head and swung it straight down on the fish that snuggled against the rock near his left sneaker.

Pow!

He clobbered it! Clobbered it good! Then, before the water settled, he swung at the next one, on his right, harboring under a ledge of rock. The club broke the water at an angle.

Crunch!

One by one Skeeter massacred the fish. Some gave him sport, zipping around in a frenzy of churned water, but the pool was small, the perimeter contained, and soon only one remained. It tried creeping along the edge of the rocks but there was nowhere to hide. Skeeter herded it into a crevice and, carefully closing in with the splintery end of the stick, speared it as he had the mouse in the garbage can. And like the mouse when he finished pressing and twisting, the fish stuck on the stick when he lifted it.

Out of the water, the perch flashed golden in the sunlight. Skeeter smiled at the unexpected dazzle, then whipped the stick as if cracking a whip. Spinning end over end, the fish flew into the trees.

BY THE TIME STEVEN GOT HOME, THE SHADOW OF THE oak on the front lawn stretched halfway across Buena Vista Drive. Not that he was in a hurry for Mom and Dad to see his black eye; early or late, he was going to catch hell. His lateness couldn't be helped. After Skeeter stomped off, Billy Bob hadn't let Whitey and him go but made them go hiking with him and Mauser.

Billy led them north past Dixie Highway till they came to another, bigger creek that ran through the fields and woods behind people's yards. They stayed away from people, and when they got close to town, they followed the train tracks till they came out on Peabody Road a half mile north of Billy's house.

All the while, Steven had felt that Mauser, who led the way, eyeballing everything with his tongue hanging out, was a walking time bomb. Tired as he was, he'd felt an immense gratitude when they came to Billy's house and Billy finally let them go.

Whitey left him a short while later, turning up the dirt road that led to his cabin, still looking as if he was in shock and dreading facing his parents so much Steven was tempted to ask him over to his house for dinner, except it was past dinner time and there'd be Cain raised in his own house when his dad saw his eye.

Before parting, Whitey had broken down and cried. Earlier, when he'd related last night's events, he'd spoken in sobs and his eyes had watered; but now, away from Billy Bob and Skeeter, he wept freely. Standing on the dusty side of the road, Whitey mourned his slain hero. "Jimmy's dead," he croaked, shaking his head in disbelief. "He was the only one who ever liked me...I miss him!"

The plaintive appeal of Whitey's bloodshot eyes was heart-wrenching. Fighting his emotions to keep his own eyes dry, Steven put an arm around the smaller boy, who leaned his forehead against Steven's shoulder and shook with the violence of his grief. When Steven reached home, his tee shirt was still wet.

Sun'll be setting soon, he thought as he walked up the drive. And then what? Would someone else die tonight? A wintery chill blew across his spine. And what if the killer came after him? If Jimmy couldn't save himself, what were his chances? Only thing he could do was run. And what about Mikey, who shared his room? The killer had gone after Whitey when he'd finished with Jimmy. What was to stop him from taking Mikey too?

Lamar Little...

That part was hard to swallow. Too hard. Whitey had to be confused. Whitey himself had said the killer was covered with quicksand and blood; surely it would be hard to recognize somebody with mud on his face.

He thought of Lance and the little girl Skeeter had told them about. Their hearts had been stolen. In his darkest imagination he heard the sound of breaking ribs and put his hand over his heart, as if to warm a cold spot that had taken root there.

Mikey must've heard him come in, because here he came,

stampeding down the hall, yelling, "Steee-viee! Me an' Mom's makin' cookieees!"

Steven said, "Hi, Mikey." Mikey's eyes went big when he saw him. And then he was flying back down the hall yelling at the top of his lungs, "Stevie got a black eye! Stevie got a black eye!" And in two seconds, Mom and Dad were confronting him—Mom with her baking glove on, Dad with his ballpoint pen in one hand, crossword puzzle in the other—gaping at the damage.

"Oh, sweet Jesus!" Mom exclaimed.

"Who did this to you?" Dad demanded.

They said other things, but it was all a din to his ears. Then, all of a sudden, he thought it was funny, as if their lips were moving and they weren't saying anything at all, and he smiled and said, "Hi, everybody. Sorry I missed supper." That quieted Mom and Dad, because if you were well enough to worry about supper, you couldn't be hurt too badly.

"Wow! Pow! Bam!" Mikey exploded in front of his face, swinging his pink little fists in the air. Steven smiled and nodded: these were among the first words Mikey had learned to read from his Bat Man comics because they were the ones printed the largest.

"Yeah, Mikey! Pow! Crash! Kablooie!" He made an exploding gesture with his hands.

"Kablooie!" Mikey shouted exuberantly, imitating the gesture. Steven would have laughed if his eye didn't hurt so.

"Oh, dear," Mom said.

"Mikey, go back in the kitchen and help your mom finish making those cookies."

"Cookies!" Mikey yelled.

"Oh, they've got a few more minutes to bake," Mom said. "I just turned the pan around."

"Katherine, I'd like to talk to Stevie about his accident."

"'Accident,' my big toe," Mom said, examining his eye; but she took Mikey by the hand and led him back to the kitchen.

"Well, Son?" Dad said when they were alone.

"I...had a fight with Skeeter."

"Skeeter?"

"Francis Mulligan."

"I think I ought to have a talk with the boy's father." Dad started toward the phone which occupied the small table in the hall.

"Don't, Dad!"

"Eh? Why?"

"Because I gave him a black eye too." Steven cringed inside. *Uh oh, here it comes: the two wrongs don't make a right lecture.*

But Dad only smiled and settled into a chair. "Did you now?"

And only now, seeing Dad's smile, did Steven realize the enormity of what he'd done. He hadn't run; he had fought back. And Dad was proud of him.

He felt better.

For a while.

Until he remembered Jimmy was dead.

And the sun was setting.

ALL DAY THE SUNLIGHT HAS PRESSED LIKE AN IRON weight on the water over the quicksand, a ponderous tombstone to keep the dead from rising. Even now, as the orange light slants from the setting sun, the weight is unbearable, suffocating.

The sun sets. The light bleeds from the sky, fades to twilight. The stars come out above the dead, lightning-scarred tree. Mist curls over the surface of the creek.

Beneath the mist, the water stirs. And if a sharp-eyed owl or jay were watching from a branch of the ancient cypress, it might see a hand emerge, followed by a head that spews a long scintillant arc of sand and water from its mouth; might see the small, ravaged carcass leap from the pit. But no bird watches. Birds have given the area a wide berth for many a year.

The rotting, waterlogged corpse begins walking, stiffly at first, then more spryly, finally loping, its leprous feet slicing through the water and white mist.

SKEETER'S TREE HOUSE—WHICH HAD BEGUN THREE years ago as a platform and some short boards nailed to the tree for climbing—was in a copse of trees on the far side of the pea field that lay behind Pa's property. Eventually, Skeeter had added walls and a roof, dragging in boards and nails of various dimensions, and, finally, he had covered the roof and two of the walls with an old canvas tarpaulin he'd found moldering and stiff in a pile of garbage somebody'd dumped on the side of a dirt road. In time, he had dispensed with the board ladder and had hung a knotted rope that could be hauled up behind him and had tacked an old blue bathrobe over the entrance.

By spending the night in the tree house, he hoped to outsmart the killer. Let the fool go to his house where he'd have to reckon with Pa and his big brothers. Skeeter smiled at the image of some dopey kid covered with mud and making believe he was Lamar Little walking in and trying to scare Pa and Luke and Ernie.

Two things he'd brought with him to the tree house: a hurricane lantern, which sat on the floor dialed down to a small flame, and Ernie's buck knife, which he'd snuck out of Ernie's closet. Skeeter didn't believe in Bloody Bones or in ghosts, but if somebody came creeping around the tree house tonight, he planned on sticking him. He'd vowed to himself that he would stay awake all night, but like every promise he had ever made, he hadn't kept it.

He dreamed of the fish. Seeing himself standing like a god over the cowering perch, he speared the fish trying to hide under the edge of a rock and brought up a mouse squirming on the end of his stick. The mouse had Billy Bob's face. He hurled it into the trees.

I Bloody Bones, an' I comin' to get you.

"Go way..." he muttered, waking. The flame in the hurricane lantern was dying. He reached to turn it up, but it sputtered and went out.

Skee-ter.

Skeeter listened, suddenly wide awake. Had someone called his name? He gripped the bone handle of the knife and felt his way to the door. He had matches but he didn't want to stick his head out with a light shining behind him. Patting the wall, Skeeter found the big nail just inside the entrance.

The rope's gone! Oh shit!

Kneeling on one knee, he whisked the terry cloth door aside with the knife.

No one was there—least not right outside the door. Neither was the rope. That angered Skeeter—that somebody had stolen something that belonged to *him*. Cautiously, he peered out.

The woods were all black and white—splashes of white moonlight against a background of velvet blackness. Seeing nothing in the lighted spaces below, he squinted to penetrate the shadows.

There! Somebody was standing in the shadow of a nearby tree. Skeeter felt the cold clutch of fear. It did not escape him that the figure was about Lamar's size.

Come out and play, Skeeter. Or are you chicken? The shadow didn't move, but he heard the message loud and clear, bouncing off the inside of his skull.

Skeeter stuck his head farther out to yell, "I ain't no chicken!" but only got up to "I ain't—" before he realized he hadn't heard the voice with his ears. Gooseflesh crawled over his skin.

Inside my head!

And on the heels of that: *It's a trick! Some kinda fancy voice throwin'.*

"You hear me down there?" he shouted. "I'm gonna stick you, Boy!"

If I can find a way down.

Skeeter heard a buzzing and wondered if a hive of bees had set up near his tree house. He looked up. There was the rope, still tied to the next branch up; only it coiled about the limb like a vine clinging to bark. The knot was just above. He reached up and tugged the rope. As if it were glued to the tree, it wouldn't budge. His flesh prickled. The bugger had been up here! Why hadn't he come into the tree house while he was sleeping and cut his throat?

Sticking the knife in his belt, Skeeter grabbed the branch, swung out and up, threw a leg over, and was sitting astride the limb in a wink. He planned to work his way out on the limb, find the end of the rope, then crawl back, ripping the rope free as he went.

The dark figure below still hadn't moved, and Skeeter wondered if he was mistaking a shadow for an assailant and the killer was in the tree. He looked up. Fear slid down his back like a handful of ice-cold razor blades as his gaze traveled along the moonlit branches. Satisfied that he was alone in the tree, he smirked at the shadow and thought, *Bit off more'n you can chew, ain'tcha, snot?*

We'll see, came the silent reply, and Skeeter broke out in a cold sweat. His bulb might not be the brightest around, but he was smart enough to realize the dark shape had read his thoughts.

Suddenly, the rope whipped around his ankle and yanked him off the branch. He screamed as the ground rushed up in a savage blur.

Then he was rebounding, flying up and up until he was almost level with the branch; and then, as if whatever force had lifted him had suddenly let go, he plummeted. Spinning upside down at the end of the rope, his body described a great pendulum arc interrupted halfway through by the trunk of the stout oak. The sound of Skeeter's head bursting open when it slammed into the tree echoed through the moonlit woods like the chop of a woodman's ax.

Dripping brains and blood, Skeeter's body settled into a diminishing circle. The Dark Man stepped from the shadow. The cool white moonlight shown uncompromisingly on his upturned visage. Silently, the Dark Man laughed.

Or almost silently: the air vibrated with the buzzing of flies that matted his hair and crawled over his flesh.

The buzzing grew louder as the insects boiled off the old corpse and settled on the new.

SEVENTEEN

T*here's only two kinds of critters in this world,* he heard Pa say, *lions and sheep. And by God, I ain't raised no sheep!*

Yes, Pa.

Billy Bob's head hurt. He had always thought of himself as a lion, or a bear, or at least as King of the Mountain. He had lost something. What was it? He had never been any good at expressing his feelings, not even to himself. In his dream state, his subconscious showed him what he had lost.

You don't feel well because your spine's comin' unglued, Son. You'd be amazed how short you'd be without a spine.

And he saw himself slithering on the floor like a fat spineless slug.

Don't cringe, Boy! I ain't raised no damned jelly fish!

Except for being wary of Pa's anger, Billy had pretty much been a stranger to fear. But he knew fear now. Intimately. If he had to pinpoint the moment in which fear had gripped him, he'd have to say it was when he'd seen the flies working in the flesh of Lamar's wounds. Buzzing, crawling, feeding...

The flies made the difference between thinking of death in a story-book way ("And then the brave knight died.") and seeing the cold, unnerving reality of the bleeding, flyblown cadaver. He could still smell the blood—pungent and hot, as vivid as the smack of his father's belt.

In the palm of his hand, he felt something warm, wet, and slimy, soft as a handful of maggots—a foulness that reeked of blood and a strong shit stink. The muscles on his back jumped with horror as if skinned serpents slithered over them.

Billy Bob woke, sat bolt upright as if Pa had yanked him by the ear. The dream scattered like shredded photographs tossed to the wind. A thin whine escaped him as he examined his hand. The hand was empty, but the overpowering stink hung in the air.

The window was wide open, and on the sill something glistened wetly in the starlight.

CURSING, LUTHER THREW OFF HIS BEDSPREAD, BILLY Bob's scream ringing in his ears.

"Goddamn you, Boy!" he roared. He grabbed his belt and headed to Billy's room. "If you're cryin', I'm gonna strop the tar outta you!"

Only when he was pushing open Billy Bob's door did he remember that two of Billy's pals had been murdered in the night and that the same thing might now be happening to Billy. For a fleeting second, he wished he'd brought his service weapon instead of a strap. Then the door was open and there was Billy, sitting up in bed, white as a ghost, pointing. His bottom lip trembled, but he made no effort to speak.

Luther's gaze followed the shaking finger. The smell hit him even before he saw the glistening rope of bloody intestine that sagged over the sill of the open window and hung down onto the floor. Rounding the bed, his mouth dry as sawdust, he went to the window. Careful not to touch the steaming entrails, he poked his head cautiously over the sill.

The dark, gutted shape was right below, lying in the petunia patch, staring back at the stars with glazed, unseeing eyes. Pale wisps of steam rose from the gaping abdominal cavity where hot intestines contacted the cooler night air.

"Mauser!" Luther whispered incredulously. Anger tightened his jaw. He glanced about the yard but saw no one lurking in the shadows.

He pulled his head back into the room, closed the window tight on the entrails and locked it. Mauser's corpse was as fresh as he'd seen. The killer couldn't be far away if he was on foot.

Might even be in the house.

"Stay here!" he ordered Billy, who still stood on the bed with his spare tire bulging over the elastic of his skivvies. Luther closed the door and headed back to his room and got his revolver and a flashlight. He turned on the hall light and went into the kitchen, shoving open the door and leaping into the room with the flashlight off. The door crashed against the wall. Flicking on the flashlight, he swept the beam under the table, over the far side of the room by the stout King Cool refrigerator. Satisfied, he pulled the light cord and hurried out the back door.

No footprints met his beam on the steps. The moon had set, but the stars were out in force and the kitchen window threw a white trapezoid into the yard. As he gave the corner of the house a wide berth, he realized the katydids were silent.

The flower bed that only Mrs. Wallace, their neighbor and part-time housekeeper, kept up was a blood bath. Luther played his beam over the carcass.

"Jesus," he muttered, tightening his grip on the revolver. Mauser had been opened up good—not only were his guts exposed but also his throat was cut.

Glancing through the window, he saw Billy sitting on his bed watching him. As he stepped past the carcass, something caught his eye. He played the beam over the grass for a moment and then he saw it—blood on the grass, dabs leading away from Mauser. He bent to examine the first of these.

Footprints. The killer had gotten blood on the soles of his bare feet. The hair crept on his arms and the back of his neck as he took in the smallness of the tracks.

The prints quickly grew fainter and vanished. Luthor glanced around to see that no one was sneaking up on him, then he held the flashlight close to the ground and let the beam play horizontally over the short stubbly grass. The light cast a shadow where the grass had been freshly crushed. There were more of the small, child-sized prints ahead. They led toward the front of the house. He rose and followed.

His front door, he saw when he rounded the corner, was wide open. Splotches of wet sand mounted the green-painted risers. Halfway up the steps he stopped when the hall light flickered and went out. Billy's light was still on; but Luther didn't notice, for he was staring at the thing sprawled on the hall floor.

The boy lay face down with one arm crooked beneath him. Even on the porch, the stench wafting through the open door told him he was looking at a corpse. Holding the Eveready in one hand and his Smith & Wesson in the other, Luther cautiously advanced.

Inside the door, he swung the beam around, searching for any sign of another person. Satisfied that he and the corpse were alone in the hall, he stepped closer, breathing shallowly to minimize the awful stench.

Lavonne Little had given him a snapshot of her boy Lamar taken within the year and Luther had briefly looked on the boy's face before wrapping him in the tarpaulin, so although the mauling and exposure to quicksand had taken their toll, he had no doubt in his mind that he was looking at the remains of Lamar Little.

He shown the flashlight on the neck wound, disturbing flies that had settled there. A black swamp leech protruding from the hole vanished down the dead boy's throat. Luther wondered what other abominations were living in the carcass. He had seen worse sights in Korea, but not many.

Luther wasn't familiar enough with fear to recognize the eerie feeling that crept over him. If he'd thought about it, he would have guessed he was coming down with a touch of fever. Holding his breath, he bent to turn the corpse over.

At that moment Billy Bob's door opened, spilling light into the hall. Luthor looked up in time to see Billy appear, pale and gaping in the doorway—and missed the movement at his feet as the corpse stabbed upwards with the knife it had concealed beneath it.

Billy's eyes widened. Following his son's gaze, Luthor stared in wonder at the big butcher knife sticking out of his chest and the scarlet river running down to his boxer shorts.

BILLY SLAMMED THE DOOR ON THE VISION OF LAMAR Little's face, sandy drool running from the corners of its grinning mouth, hell fire glowing balefully in its sunken eyes. As he crammed his bulk under his bed, he heard Pa hit the floor. Moments later, as he struggled with the shrieks of hysteria that threatened to erupt, he heard the sound of splintering bone.

And when the smacking, slurping noises began, he did scream—shriek after gibbering shriek following him into darkness as he lost consciousness and the mad laughter howled down the hall.

EIGHTEEN

Through the veil of flames, Mauvis watched the corpse of the dead boy, Lamar Little, crouching in the shadow of the tree.

Finding the corpse had been easy; Mrs. Little had left her the boy's tee shirt. Within the feverish orange glow of the embers, the corpse appeared to her as a black silhouette. But she could tell what it was doing by the way it raised its hands to its mouth and the head twisted as if its teeth were tearing.

It was eating. Though she had penetrated the mystery more deeply than most, the thought of the dead eating shocked her.

And what do the dead eat?

She knew the answer, didn't she? Even out here on the edge of the swamp, the news traveled.

Some crazy person cut their hearts out.

Trembling, suspecting the power that animated the dead child and sated monstrous appetites, she concentrated on the corpse's face until it filled her vision.

The hickory staff slipped from her hand, clattered on the hearthstone.

He's back! But how?

She'd bound him to a plowshare and sunk him in quicksand, but somehow Celia's killer was back. And wearing Lamar Little's body.

It came to her how it might have happened. Whoever removed the child's body from the meadow had thrown it into the same quicksand hole as—

With the suddenness of an animal knowing it's being watched, the corpse froze, hand to mouth, and looked up from the glowing embers. Its black eyes found hers and its dead lips stretched in a bloody grin.

1924

For days after seeing the killer in the embers, Mauvis had worried what to do. Go to the police? She could just picture that.

"Yes, an' where'd you say you saw this fella kill your daughter?"

"In the fire."

A funny look as if she was tetched. "You a moonshiner, Girl?"

Yes, indeed, that's about how it would go if she went to the law. Besides, she wanted to hurt this man herself, make him suffer, as he had made Celia suffer.

She had gone the very night of her seeing and found Celia's body, had brought her home and stitched her wounds and bathed her. Celia was buried in the colored cemetery on Magnolia Street. Mauvis was surprised at the turnout for the funeral. Who would ever have thought so many people, whites as well as blacks, would show up for the funeral of a hoodoo woman's daughter? But then they hadn't come for Celia alone; they had congregated because Celia was the fourth child that month to be found dead and butchered, and two others were missing. The mourners had gathered to express their collective grief.

Soon after the funeral, she took to going down to Mr. Jacob's grocery store to buy a nickel grape Nehi and drink it on the bench right outside the screen door where she could hear the folks who came in to shop and gossip talk over the counter with Mr. Jacob. Sitting there in the shade under the metal awning that ran the length of the storefront, staring out at the heat waves rising off the dusty road simmering in the glaring sunlight, now and then touching the soda pop to her lips just enough to wet her mouth, she listened and waited. In this way, she learned that the tall stranger who had butchered her baby had come up from Florida three months ago and rented a piece of land to farm from Mr. Hanson.

Of course, the main topic of conversation among the men and women who drifted in and out of Mr. Jacob's was the disappearances and the bodies found and speculation as to what the killer was doing with the hearts he carved from his victims' corpses.

On the third straight day that she came into the store, she was standing near the register and Mr. Jacob was handing her

her change, when the screen door opened and there he was, tall and so dark he was almost black and nearly handsome—*nearly* because, even though he was smiling, his eyes dark and haughty, she could see beneath the cool veneer the twisted mask of pleasure and madness she had seen in the fire, as spittle had drooled from his lips and he had choked the life from her seven-year-old daughter. Her change slipped from her hand, clattered on the glass countertop.

Feeling his eyes crawling over her body, she picked up her nickel and, wishing Mr. Jacob a pleasant day, left the store. It was all she could do to control herself, to keep from walking over to Mr. Jacob's butcher block, picking up his meat cleaver, and stepping up behind the animal and burying the polished steel in his skull.

And what would she tell the judge when he asked her what evidence she had to prove he was the man who had killed her Celia.

But your honor, I saw it in the fire.

Once out the door—terrified that he might start talking to her when he came out and she would ruin everything—she hurried home, carrying the soda pop with her, forgetting the penny deposit on Mr. Jacob's bottle.

Back home, she considered killing him with hoodoo, dressing nine black candles in bad vinegar and writing the name of her daughter's murderer on each candle with needles singed in a frying pan. The candles she would burn one each for nine days, biting off the bottoms and lighting them at that end with the stub of the previous candle to hasten his destruction. But merely killing him wasn't enough; she wanted to see him die, wanted to see the life go out of his eyes as he writhed in agony at her feet. She—not the law, not John Flowers, not nobody but Mauvis Mae Flowers—would kill this monster, this murderer and mutilator of children. Oh yes, she wanted to see the hate in his eyes as he died knowing it was she who killed him!

After that, she took to walking in the dirt lane that passed before the shanty he'd rented. For these occasions, she dressed not in the somber house dresses she had worn since her husband left her during the war for a white woman in France, but in a new blue calico dress that emphasized the curve of her hips and cork-soled sandals. Next to her heart, she wore a small silk bag into which she had sewn white mustard seed for protection against harm and steel dust filed from the end of a horse-shoe magnet to draw him to her, and for good measure, she had splashed herself liberally with Cleo-May perfume, guaranteed to compel a man's desire.

The second day she did this, he was waiting for her by his mailbox, admiring her and smiling broadly as she approached. She noted his broad shoulders, his high cheek-bones, his teeth and the whites of his eyes blazing against the darkness of his flesh. His shirt and hands were clean. He certainly hadn't been working in the field. She doubted he even owned a mule and a plow.

She neither stopped nor answered nor glanced his way when he greeted her, but walked on, eyebrows arched, lips pursed, her gaze haughty, disinterested.

He followed and fell in beside her. Outwardly, she took no notice, but inwardly, sized him up out of the corner of her eye. She was tall; he was taller: over six feet, maybe two hundred pounds and all of it lean muscle.

"Is your heart as cold as your eyes, Girl?" he said.

She stopped and, using all the art she could muster to sustain the coquettish smile while inwardly seething, she said, "Colder," and continued walking.

"Umm. Nothing like a cold woman on a hot day," he said, keeping up with her.

It was working. She had never been the coquettish type, but she knew the effect a cool hen could have on a hot rooster. When she turned off the road and started across a field, he invited himself along, chatting about how he planned to fix up the shanty roof before the winter rains came and how, come next spring, he planned on planting watermelon and tobacco.

"Where we heading?" he asked.

"*I'm* heading home," she said.

"Say, you the one live in that cabin back there?" He nodded toward the pine trees across the field. "Near the swamp?"

Panic clutched her. Had he been watching her house? She stumbled and he reached to steady her, but with a lithe movement, she eluded him.

"That's where I live," she said, forcing herself to sound bored. "It was my Granny's place; she left it to me."

"Is your husband home?"

She glanced at him and let the devil show in her smile as she strolled along the grass-grown bank of an irrigation ditch. "My husband died in France during the war," she lied. The lie was the official story she offered anyone who asked why John Flowers hadn't returned from fighting the Hun. It made him out a hero, but better that than the humiliation of public knowledge of her desertion.

"Ah, a widow." Then, after a silence: "Any young'uns?"

"No, no children." She concentrated on keeping her hands from shaking.

Beyond the field, they came upon a well-trod path that led through the woods not only to her property but also to some of the best fishing holes in the county. When they came to her place, he paused on the front lawn to take in the bee hives and then the house itself.

"You going to invite me in?" he said, his smile returning basilisk-like. "Perhaps offer me a glass of tea?"

She gazed at him through heavy lashes mascaraed for the first time since 1916, the year John left for France. A sardonic smile played upon her rouged lips. "I didn't think you'd be gentleman enough to wait until I asked."

He came up the steps to her without saying a word, just smiling. And though there was a hardness, a cruelty, in his eyes, in his arrogant grin, she could see how some women would be attracted to him. But she had seen his drooling, flustered face as he'd raped and strangled Celia. Had seen his mad eyes rolled back in his head as he'd eaten her heart. She hurried into the less bright interior of the cabin to hide the pain in her face. He pushed in through the screen door behind her.

"Nice place," he said after taking a look around as if to satisfy himself no one else was home. "Your husband make this?" He was admiring her pine cupboard.

"Yes." She didn't hate John for leaving her with child, not anymore. Nor did she hate him for not being here to help her murder this man; she wanted that pleasure for herself.

The stranger came up behind her as she'd expected he would and put his hands on her shoulders.

Please dear God, she prayed. *Don't let him feel my disgust.*

The top button of her dress was open and he slipped a finger under her collar and felt the curve of her shoulder muscle. His touch was light, sensuous. "You have beautiful skin," he said and bent his lips to her shoulder.

It had been a long, warm walk and she could feel the sweat trickling between her breasts, her cotton dress clinging to her back. The heat of his mouth at the base of her throat burned her. She slipped away. Flashing him a (hopefully) seductive smile, she headed for the kitchen. "Why don't you sit on the porch. It's cooler out there. I'll get us some tea."

When she returned with the glasses, he was sitting on the edge of her bed, his eyes brashly watching her walk. His eyes were bold; they bore right through her, undressed her, and used her. When he took the glass, he held her hand and kept it captive as he tilted the cool tea to his lips. She reached for him, her fingers curling around his neck, and she gazed smokily into his eyes.

His lips were smiling, but she glimpsed in his eyes something as cold as the ashes in her hearth. A serpent uncoiling, a dragon stretching. She reminded herself that he was addicted to killing the way others were addicted to liquor.

Does he plan to kill me too? she wondered as she strolled over to the table, saucily emphasizing the sway of her hips, feeling his gaze on her back. She was glad she had taken the precaution of hiding John the Conqueror Root in the four corners of the cabin to give her the upper hand. Taking another sip, she sat her glass on the table. Now she moved toward the hearth, still feeling the heat of his gaze as he sipped his tea and watched her from the bed. She had concealed a knife on top of the mantle behind the big orange pottery vase that held an assortment of dried wildflowers and grasses.

Just in case.

"I heard the men down at Mr. Jacob's grocery store say you was from Florida, that right?"

"Yes."

"I never been to Florida. I heard about palm trees; what're they like?"

"Well...they're tall and got branches like big feathers; sort of like those ferns—" He pointed to the dried fronds arranged fanlike in the vase that hid the knife. "—only big as tree limbs."

He rose and walked over to her, his stride catlike, arrogant. Her heart lurched when he reached toward the mantlepiece, but he only set down his glass.

He slid his hands around her waist. "You're trembling," he said. Serpents coiled in his eyes.

Affecting amusement, she flashed him a sultry glance. "A little, I guess. Ain't every day I invite a handsome man into my home."

His smile broadened, as she had hoped it would. She could smell the pungent aromatic scent of him. He swooped to kiss her. She turned her head so that his lips found her cheek. He started to turn her mouth toward his, but she forced his head down. "Yes, right there." She managed an appropriate giggle as his lips nestled into the crook of her shoulder at the base of her neck. His tongue moved slowly at first, tasting, then faster, devouring her as he drew her to him, pressing her tight against his chest. His left hand, hot through the damp calico, slid down her back, squeezed her buttocks.

Get away! she told herself, starting to panic in the claustrophobic embrace.

And then he bit her!

His arms were tight around her. Her own arms were pinned between them. He bit her in the muscle at the base of her neck, bit her hard. She felt the skin puncture as she cried out. She worked a hand free and shoved it under his chin. His head snapped back, but he didn't let go. With her one free hand, she groped wildly over his shoulder for the knife. The vase toppled, crashed on the hearthstone.

Laughing, he swung her around, held her at arm's length. There was a mad light in his eyes (the serpents were loose!) and a speck of blood on his white teeth.

Get away!

His hand came up to caress her face. "So pretty. So very pret—"

She ducked, slipped out of his grasp. Grinning, he stepped toward her—and went down on one knee, his face a sudden grimace of pain. He clutched his gut. Comprehension dawned on him, transforming his expression into one of rage—rage so intense his gums showed, his eyes bulged, and the veins stood out like ropes in his neck.

"You poisoned me, witch!" he bellowed.

A savage, humorless grin twisted her face as she backed away. "Not yet, you bastard! But soon. Soon. Getting hard to move, ain't it?"

Then she was turning to run, because he was reaching round behind him, grabbing up a hunk of firewood and hurling it at her all in one blurred motion.

He was resisting the Deadly Nightshade she'd slipped into his tea. The cedarwood length clipped her a glancing blow behind the ear and the room became overwhelmingly bright as she pitched forward onto her hands and knees.

He pounced, lifting her by her hair. His hands found her throat. She fought him tooth and nail, but the blow to her head left her disoriented and weak. She cried now, and through the veil of tears, she saw his face as she had seen it the night she watched him strangle Celia: eyes bulging, teeth bared, a ropy strand of spittle gleaming from his lower lip. She smelled the jasmine tea on his rasping breath...the poisoned honey. His skin gleamed with sweat, as his fingers tightened on her neck, thumbs crushing her windpipe.

Her vision swam. As if the roof were gone and the sun had moved closer to the earth, the room grew intolerably bright. His face floated in the light. This close up, she could tell where his dark brown, almost black irises left off and his pupils began. She was swooning... falling... dropping endlessly down a black shaft. Images, smells, sounds, savage emotions rushed at her from the blackness, swept like a wind through her mind, tearing at her reason the way a twister tears off roof shingles—ripping them up and spinning them away.

She saw images of murder and madness. She saw corpses, children mostly, rotting in field and in swamp, not even hidden but arrogantly left lying where he had finished with them. She saw him sometimes dressed in that dark suit, pretending to be a preacher, other times wild and naked in the woods, bathing in blood and howling at the moon. She heard the splintering of ribs and saw the spurting hearts carved, in some instances still beating, from the chest. She saw a pentagram drawn in blood on the hard earth, a severed human head at each point. Words she heard, in his voice, only loud and beseeching, and though the tongue was foreign, she recognized in their rhythms and in their context the patterns of ritual magic.

Sensations.

Images.

Horror.

Then the light was dimming, the images slowing, petering out. Pinpricks of light swarmed like gnats in the darkness. She felt a release and wondered if her soul was leaving her body, answering the Lord's call. But then her vision was clearing and she blinked and he was on the floor beside her. His hands still clutched her throat, but he was paralyzed and she was alive! She pushed herself up. The floor tilted. She shoved his hands away, slapped his face, spat on him.

His face was a mask of purple rage.

"I am bocor!" he hissed between clenched teeth in a thick West Indian accent. His voice was full of the chaffing of dry snakeskins, of the skittering of dead leaves. "I will come back for you. You think you have killed me? I tell you I will live and *you* shall die!"

Those were his last words, because the next moment he made a croaking noise and his eyes bulged as his face darkened, and with a surge of savage joy she realized the paralysis had reached his throat and he could no longer breathe.

She watched him die, curled on the floor, his strong brown hands reduced to arthritic claws, his tongue protruding, purpling. Soon, as she had promised, the life faded from his eyes, left them flat and vacant and dead.

When Mauvis calmed enough to think again, she poured bad vinegar into the corpse's mouth and sprinkled in goofer dust—not from just any grave but dirt gathered from Celia's resting place—and red pepper and closed its mouth with a packet of needles soaked in vinegar while she beseeched God and the four winds to condemn the monster's soul to eternal agony within its rotting corpse. This done, she dragged the body out back and secured it and her iron plowshare onto Claudie, the mule she'd had in those days; and leading Claudie into the swamp, did her best to keep the bocor from keeping his promise.

NINETEEN

The next morning, when Luther failed to show up for work and repeated calls to his house went unanswered, TJ drove out to see what was going on. The front door was open and the house looked deserted when TJ pulled in behind the Sheriff's car.

The bloody, child-sized footprints leading across the porch and down the front steps confirmed the premonition that had gripped him during the drive until he'd broken out in a cold sweat and pushed the speedometer over ninety. He drew his revolver before pushing through the screen door.

The hall was pregnant with the blood scent—a thick, coppery smell that reminded him of watching his pa and grand pa slaughter pigs, hauling the three-hundred-pound porkers up by their hind legs and then axing them in the throat. He remembered the blood pooling on the ground, too thick to soak into it easily, and the inevitable flies greedily sucking the earth. The sight in Luther's hall was similar, even to the flies that crawled over the red-splashed floor boards and the corpse. Luther lay on his back gaping wide-eyed at the ceiling, his shirt torn to shreds, the hole in his chest yawning bloodily, splintered ribs protruding at odd angles.

TJ rushed forward.

And then he was diving, throwing himself against the wall, low to the floor. A deafening roar filled the hall. He felt the air behind him part. Another blast shook the air. A section of doorjamb disintegrated. Splinters lodged in his shoulder.

TJ got to his feet. Billy Bob stood in a bedroom doorway. The shotgun's double barrels swung toward him, tracking him as he backed into a wall. TJ's mouth was too dry to speak though his lips shaped a voiceless *No!*

The click of hammers falling on empty chambers was deafening.

THAT AFTERNOON, TJ VISITED MRS. MAUVIS FLOWERS.

Billy had been taken to the hospital in Caledonia, and TJ had turned the investigation over to the State Police. They were equipped for a thorough investigation; the Farnsworth Sheriff's Department was not. Still, after two hours with Captain Connelly, going over the particulars surrounding the murders and watching the lab boys dust for fingerprints and take blood samples, pointing out similarities between some of the cases—hearts missing, a child's footprints—he'd gone back to the office to continue some research of his own.

"Whoo-wee!" Lyle exclaimed.

"What?" TJ lowered the yellowed newspaper he'd been scanning to hear what Lyle had found. They sat in the break room, the ledgers and newspapers they'd been researching much of yesterday spread between them on the Formica-topped table.

"Listen to this."

TJ picked up his pen and pulled his yellow legal pad from under the newspaper.

"'September 27, 1924,'" Lyle read off the top of the page, then scanned down until he found his place. "A skull was turned up by two boys playin' truant. Mmm. Found it by the creek near Peabody Road. Mmm." TJ endured the monotonous noise Lyle made to mark his deletions as he scanned down a paragraph or two. "'Yesterday, an organized search turned up two nearly intact bodies, tentatively identified as Jo Beth Dearling and Tracy Tudor, aged seven and nine, missing since early August.

"'Also discovered were three additional skulls and a variety of skeletal remains. When sorted out, County authorities estimated the collection to represent the remains of as many as seven victims. Said Major Clarence Drake of the County Police Department, "There is no evidence of beheading. We believe that the absence of the other skulls is natural and that they were carried off by predators.' Mmm... Hearts were missing from the two corpses."

Besides reading to each other and taking notes, they'd compiled a list of people who had given testimony to the police and the CALEDONIA CRIER. Lyle's memory was almost as good as Mrs. Greentree, the librarian's. Lyle had trimmed the list to five.

Mauvis Flowers, who had lost a daughter to the murderer

who'd stalked Farnsworth in 1924, was the third person he visited. She would have been the last considering he had to leave his station wagon where the dirt road dead-ended and continue on foot, but Trish McCormick was laid up in the hospital with a broken hip and Bud Miller was fishing down Panama City.

As a boy, TJ and his buddies used to sneak up to the edge of the trees and spy on her house and throw dirt bombs on her sheets hanging out to dry (as he imagined kids still did today). She was the hoodoo woman, and speculation had run rampant as to what she did to kids she caught. On the few occasions he'd seen her since he'd become deputy, he'd decided she looked more level-headed than most of the folks around, white or black, only quieter and more reclusive than was considered normal. Now that he knew about her tragedy, he reckoned she had reason for her sad eyes and life of seclusion.

Mrs. Flowers was standing on her porch when he arrived. He had the eerie feeling she'd been waiting for him. She didn't invite him in and their brief conversation was conducted standing, with him in the yard and her at the top of the steps, though there were two serviceable-looking chairs on her porch.

She didn't remember 1924 too well. It had been a painful year for her and she had forced herself not to think about it these thirty-some-odd years. She was sure she could provide no information that would help him. So she said. But her eyes grew wide when he mentioned that the Sheriff's heart was missing, and the whole time he spoke with her, she seemed to be struggling to keep her emotions under control. If he was any judge of people, he'd say she was hiding something. Something that was eating her up inside.

Hiking back to his car, he realized what the something else was.

She's afraid, he thought as the mosquitos hung over the path in buzzing swarms to catch the sun's dying rays.

LAMAR'S KITE WENT UP AND UP, BECAME A VAGUE GREY dot on the blue sky, vanished. And Lamar wanted to go with the kite but the dog had him by the throat. The blood spurted from the wound, spilled over the dog's jaws. Lamar's eyes rolled back in his head, glistening whites filling the sockets. His eyes kept rolling until the pupils appeared from below, as if they'd rolled all the way around. Only now his pupils were red and glowing like the embers in Mrs. Flowers' hearth.

Lamar's eyeballs burst, two jets of jelly and blood. Quicksand dribbled from the wound in his throat.

Lavonne woke screaming.

In the darkness the images continued to assault—until the curtain flung open and Rowena and Mazy followed by Granny Apple burst into the room. When she had endured their questions and anxious stares and after two tablespoons of Granny Apple's elixir ("for the nerves and to keep the nightmares away"), they left her to sleep again and Lavonne sobbed quietly into her pillow.

Reginald, forgive me! If I had known!

But she hadn't known and Reginald was dead.

Oh Lord, what have I done?

Lamar had returned. Only not Lamar. She remembered the sinister leer in his eyes, the unchildlike grin. It was as if the devil had come calling wearing Lamar's body like a suit.

Got to stop him, she thought sleepily, shock and Granny Apple's elixir dragging her under. *He'll kill others.*

But wasn't that what she'd wanted? Lamar's kite floated up and up, became a dot in the cloudless blue; the blood pool spread; her tears dried.

"Vengeance is mine, saith the Lord,'" she mumbled into her pillow. But where the Lord might take pity on Lamar's killers, she thought as she slipped into sleep, the devil would show no mercy.

TWENTY

The sun set behind the low hills that swelled gently against the horizon west of Farnsworth. The pink and gold drained from the sky and the stars emerged, hazy and twinkling in the summer humidity. In Farnsworth and in neighboring Caledonia, all but the most foolhardy locked their doors. In the swamp, the birds and dragonflies retired and the frogs and bats came out. The moon appeared, turning the mist a snowy white.

And the Dark Man rose.

BLOODY BONES STOOD AT ONE OF THE WINDOWS IN THE back of the Blankenship home, looking in. The moon, almost full, shone down on the lawn, turning night into a pale imitation of day and illuminating the room into which he stared.

The bunk bed stood just beyond the square of moonlight. Only the top bunk was occupied.

The corpse frowned, dislodging quicksand from the corners of its peeling lips. Its pupils narrowed to angry pin pricks. Steven wasn't home. The Dark Man was minded to go in and take the younger boy, but there was much to do.

He smiled, and a new tear appeared in his bottom lip as the muscle stretched. Steven could wait. He gazed at the moon for a long moment, then studied the constellations before he turned and started toward the swamp. It was a perfect night to settle an old score.

A SINGLE LIGHT SHOWED IN A WINDOW OF THE otherwise dark cabin. Squatting at the edge of the trees, Steven stroked Gator to keep her quiet while he watched the house. Fear crawled over his scalp at the thought of crossing the yard and knocking on that door under the bright moonlight, knowing that anyone looking was going to see him.

On the other hand, here he was at the edge of the woods and Lamar—"Bloody Bones," Whitey said the dead boy called himself in his dream—could be right behind him and he'd never know until it was too late. What he was doing now—contemplating going up to a stranger's house on a night when death hung in the air thick as wood smoke—was like a Bloody Bones story: an unnaturally bright moon, the dark house waiting before him with its staring windows. Like the story where you finally get to the Black House at the end of the lane and you knock on the door and ask for your mother's missing butcher knife and Bloody Bones opens up and gives you the knife—right in your chest.

Gator, who had been lying in the grass beside him, suddenly was on her feet, ears pricked. She issued a single bark that on the still night air was probably heard a mile away. Then she was sprinting for the house.

"Gator, heel!" Steven yelled and took off after her.

Gator beat him to the porch. She sat on her rump, her gaze focused on the door, her hackles bristling. A low growl issued from her throat. Steven mounted the front steps like a man going to the electric chair. "Good girl," he said and grabbed her collar. He raised his hand to knock but froze when he heard footsteps that sounded like someone in slippers approaching the door.

Or maybe it was the sound of bare dead feet shuffling over wood planks sugared with sand...

"Who?"

A woman's voice: Mrs. Little.

"S-Steven Blankenship, ma'am."

Have you seen my mother's butcher knife?

The thought came unbidden, and again he had the eerie feeling that he was living a Bloody Bones tale, acting it out to its predictable and fatal end.

"Who?"

"Steven Blankenship. Is Lamar home?"

He clapped a hand over his mouth, but too late. He'd said it. If Lamar had risen from the dead and planned to kill them all, he was the last person Steven wanted to see. He was crazy to have come here. He'd hoped his plan to find Lamar and convince him not to kill any more would make better sense on the way. It hadn't. Still, what else could he do? He'd decided he'd be better off seeking out Lamar than waiting till Lamar came looking for him.

A latch unhooked, the door opened inward, and Gator ran in growling.

A woman's startled cry and the sound of something clattering to the floor.

"Gator, heel!" Steven shouted, running in, envisioning in that half second Gator's jaws locked onto Mrs. Little's hand or leg. But Gator was only staring her down, making menacing noises deep in her throat that sounded as though they were being made by a much bigger dog.

A long, two-tined fork—the kind for turning steaks on a barbeque grill or for roasting two hot dogs at once over the kitchen stove lay nearby on the floor. The lamplight shone on the wicked-looking points. Steven scooped the weapon up, shaken that she had intended to use it on him.

"Put the dog outside." Her voice was as low and menacing as Gator's, and, like Gator, she was showing teeth. She wore a terrycloth robe over a nightgown. Her hair, grey at the roots, was frizzled and unkempt.

"I gotta find Lamar," Steven said, leaving Gator right where she was.

"Why?" The suspicion in the woman's face was unconcealed, the hatred in her eyes shocking.

"Lamar's killing people," he forced himself to say, "innocent people."

"I know; he killed his father," she said through clenched teeth.

"Then he's not dead?"

"Dead? Yes, he's dead! You and your friends killed him!"

She stabbed an accusing finger at him and damp gooseflesh broke out on his back. Gator barked and shuffled her forepaws, but Mrs. Little didn't budge.

The hallway tilted as the bedrock of his reality crumbled like so much clay. Until now, he'd had only Whitey's admittedly confused account to go by. Coming from the boy's mother, the confirmation that Lamar was dead yet still walking the earth—murdering—was shattering.

The woman's finger shook as it pointed. "You killed him! You killed my baby! You and your evil friends! You killed him just because he was black and he was happy!"

"No, it was Mauser! I ran away! I got sick! I wanted to stop it, but the blood...!" Close to tears, he felt wronged and guilty at the same time.

She wasn't hearing him. Her eyes blazed. The pointing finger curled, became part of a fist. Spittle hung from the corner of her crooked scowl as her eyes darted around as if searching for a weapon. *She wants to kill me.* The thought was chilling.

She lunged for him. He drew back and her nails scratched his chin. Snarling, Gator snapped at her and she withdrew. Steven backed away, opened the door. "Go on, Girl. Out." Gator looked from him to the woman, snarled again, then obeyed her master.

Soon as the door clicked shut behind Gator, she was on him. She tried to grab his hair, but it was too short, so she spun him around by his shoulder, his tee shirt bunched in her fist, and grabbed for the fork. He flung it clattering down the hall. She slammed him against the door. His head, snapping back, knocked against the wood and he saw stars.

"Stop it!" he screamed, crying freely as he tried to force her

off. But she was strong and full of rage, and in another moment her fingers were sliding around his throat.

"Please!" Hot tears stung his eyes. He struck out blindly, felt his palm connect resoundingly with the side of her face.

The hands released his throat. He blinked tears out of the way. The rage had gone out of her face. She touched trembling fingers to her mouth. "What am I doing?" she groaned. And then she was crying, fists pressed against the sides of her head.

SITTING ON A DAMP LOG IN THE SHADOW OF A TREE, TJ yawned and stretched. A stiff elbow popped loudly, and his narrowed gaze darted from tree to tree in the darkness behind him in case somebody had heard. Nothing moved in the woods. He heard no sound other than the ratcheting of katydids and the hoarse croaking of frogs in the nearby swamp. He took a deep breath, let it out slowly, but the tension stayed with him.

He returned his attention to the house he was staking out. The moon was so bright it lit up the lawn like the Pontiac car lot over in Caledonia. For a house with no electricity, Mrs. Flowers' place was unusually well-lit. Warm as it was, she had a fire going—smoke curled out of the chimney, drifted straight up as there was no breeze to bend it—and lantern-light showed at the three windows he could see from this angle.

He'd come here following a hunch. The woman had not

been forthcoming when he'd interviewed her. She was holding something back. Thirty years ago, her daughter had been viciously murdered, her heart carved out of her chest. That wasn't something you ever put behind you. He knew he wouldn't if it happened to one of his girls. The fear in her eyes when he'd brought up Luther's missing heart was unmistakable. And now her cabin was lit up as if she was expecting unwelcome company.

TJ looked up at the moon partly visible among the leaves. It had risen and advanced a quarter of the way up the sky since he'd started watching. The Man in the Moon, not at all his usual jovial self tonight, seemed to frown upon the earth, as if he was royally disgusted with humanity. TJ started chewing the inside of his lower lip again, stopped; the skin there was frayed. Anxiety gnawed like a rat in his guts. He should be home watching after his family. He kept seeing Luther lying in his hall covered with blood and flies, eyes and mouth gaping at the ceiling and his heart missing; and he kept thinking of going home tomorrow morning and finding his wife Sue Ann or Dotty or little Lisa in a similar predicament.

A shadow passed before one of the windows under the low eaves. A curtain parted and a face appeared. Mrs. Flowers staring out into the night. As if watching for somebody... Keeping within the shadow of the tree, he stood. He doubted all the lights and her looking out the window were due to insomnia.

The face withdrew; the curtain dropped back into place. TJ relaxed a moment, stepped away from the tree, stretched, cracked his neck.

The shock of the knife slamming into his testicles and

exiting his lower belly was so sudden, it took him a moment to realize what had happened. Then pain seared his groin as hot blood gushed down his trousers.

As nausea and incomprehension washed over him, he glimpsed the grinning corpse that yanked the knife out and stepped back. A strange thing happened as he gazed into the dead boy's mad eyes. It was as if, knowing he had only seconds left in this world, his mind chose not to dwell on the horror of his death but grasped at a fleeting image. He thought of the green-on-green Star Chief sitting on its white-walls at the Pontiac car lot over in Caledonia. Sinking to his knees, his life's blood streaming out of him, he imagined himself at the wheel and Sue Ann beside him and Dotty and Lisa happy as kittens in the back seat, chattering and pointing out the window as the Georgia pines and the dotted line flowed by.

The fat stripe of blue sky he saw in his vision darkened, the sunlight dimmed, went out, as he pitched forward onto his face.

THE DARK MAN KNELT BESIDE THE POLICEMAN'S corpse, and heedless of the spreading blood pool, was prepared to open the man's chest—when he froze, cocked his head and listened with dead ears to the sound of two people and a dog approaching. He could see them now, emerging from the trees into the moonlight: a woman and a boy.

Despite the darkness, he recognized the woman who had

ultimately provided the body he wore. Steven, he recognized by the powerful compulsion he felt to kill him and by one of the images he had found lying around in the dead boy's brain, like an abandoned marble on the floor of a dusty attic—one of six circling faces.

He watched, curious as to what would happen next, as they crossed the yard and approached the cabin.

BOTH WOMEN WERE IN TEARS. STEVEN'S OWN HAD dried and now he was possessed with a terrible sense of urgency.

And danger.

Every hair on his body was tingling. At first, he had attributed this to the terrifying trek through the woods—bats streaking low under the trees, their high squeals piercing the monotonous chorusing of the frogs—then entering the home of the one woman every kid in Farnsworth feared. Both women's stories, blurted out amid tears and emotion, were horrifying, 1956 and 1924 merging as if there had been no thirty years between, the murderer Mrs. Flowers had buried killing again in Lamar's flesh.

Steven shook his head. A fire going in the middle of July was ridiculous. The heat and the anxiety were making him dizzy. The night was passing and the killer ("bocor," Mrs. Flowers called him) might be murdering Whitey or Billy Bob this very moment.

Gator sat on one hip at the edge of the hearthstone, seemingly oblivious to the heat. She wagged her stump of a tail and watched him her brows cocked quizzically, her forehead bunched. Steven threw up his hands. "Please! Isn't there anything we can do?"

The older woman looked at him. Her brow was as furrowed as Gator's, her eyes red from crying, her expression so hopeless his heart sank. "That's just it, what I'm trying to tell you. Lamar—" Mrs. Flowers glanced at Mrs. Little "—I mean the man using Lamar's body—can't be stopped."

Steven gulped. "And that includes my death, doesn't it?"

Mrs. Flowers nodded apologetically. "Unless the body is destroyed or imprisoned."

"Oh Lord!" Mrs. Little burst into fresh tears.

Mrs. Flowers started to put her hand on the other woman's shoulder, then withdrew it. Steven stood there, not knowing what to do, cringing from the woman's outburst of emotion and feeling again the guilt that had eaten away at him all week because he had watched the woman's son die and had done nothing.

"I buried garlic and John the Conqueror Root around the cabin at the seventeen points of the world. I think we safe, but you both gotta stay here tonight." She dropped her hands to her side and barked a bitter laugh. Steven looked at her, thinking she'd lost it. The hoodoo woman shook her head. "And it's my fault. I brought the monster back."

"It's as much my fault as yours," said Mrs. Little, who had stopped crying. "I'll burn in hell for what I done, and I'll deserve it."

Gator sprang up and trotted over to the bolted front door. She stood alert, ears cocked. An ominous growl rumbled in her throat. A second later there came a knock at the door.

Steven's heart thumped at each of the two solemn raps. His gaze snapped to Mrs. Flowers, to Mrs. Little. Neither of the women moved. Then Mrs. Flowers called in a shaky voice. "Who is it?"

Gator barked.

In answer two more knocks and what sounded like a man groaning. There was something awful in the groan; the sound conveyed pain and need. Someone was hurt. Steven started for the door.

"Stay back." Mrs. Flowers went to the door. Mrs. Little joined her. The two women exchanged a nervous glance. Mrs. Little fiddled anxiously with the ruffles on the front of her white cotton dress. Gator growled again.

Again came the groan, and Steven thought he could make out words—a plea for help.

"I recognize that voice," Mrs. Little said. "It's Mr. Riley, the young deputy."

Recognition flashed in Mrs. Flowers' eyes. She nodded and unbolted the door.

"My God!" Mrs. Little cried as TJ staggered into the cabin. The women stepped back. Gator let of a fusillade of barks. Steven's jaw dropped.

Deputy Riley—whom Steven knew as the young officer who came to his class to tell him and his schoolmates how you should look both ways before crossing the street and how you should never take a ride or candy or money from a stranger—was hurt bad. From the waist down, his uniform was soaked in blood and he reeked of its hot, pungent smell.

Then Steven looked into the deputy's face and saw the grinning lips, the dead eyes slit by hideous mirth, saw the dripping butcher knife clutched in the officer's hand. The corpse's hands were filthy, caked with fresh, damp earth, and Steven realized what had happened: the bocor had killed Mr. Riley and then had used his corpse to dig up the John the Conqueror Root and to fool them into letting him in. Danger radiated from the glittering blade like the tension in the air before a thunderstorm.

The animated corpse lashed out at Mrs. Flowers. Steven fell backwards, landed hard on his rear as he tried to scramble away. Mrs. Flowers caught the knife on her staff. The blade bit into the wood with a meaty *whock*. The force of the blow drove the woman to her knees. Gator clamped her jaws on the killer's hand. The knife clattered on the floor. The bocor roared, kicked Gator in the ribs, sending the big pup sprawling into the rocking chair halfway across the room.

On her feet again, Mrs. Flowers struck the corpse a resounding knock on the skull. The deceased deputy crashed backward through the open doorway, sprawled on his back on the porch.

Mrs. Flowers rushed to close the door. Mrs. Little moved to help. The bocor was quicker. The corpse surged upward, a mass of animated meat, of mud and blood and rending hate. It kicked the door open, sending the women reeling, and drew the deputy's revolver.

"Not this time," croaked dead vocal cords as the bocor pumped two slugs into Mrs. Flowers. The first slug tore out a section of bone and hair at the old woman's temple; the second punched a hole in her heart. The hoodoo woman slammed into the floor, twitched as the life ran out of her.

Snarling, saliva flying from her trap-door mouth, Gator leapt as the barrel swung toward Mrs. Little. The dog crashed full force into the bocor's chest and sank her teeth into the dead man's throat. The bocor went down, sprawled across the porch in the patch of red firelight thrown by the roaring hearth. Gator hung on, thrashing her head as she worked more throat into her maw.

Steven's fear-paralysis broke. Snatching up Mrs. Flowers' staff, he raced out the door and laid into the downed corpse, raining a barrage of blows on the deputy's gun hand and wrist.

The revolver went off. The slug peeled wood from the cabin a foot to the right of the door. Steven's ears rang with the report.

Then a shadow cast by the firelight fell over him and he caught the glint of an axe blade uplifted and cringed as the weapon fell.

Whock!

Severing the gun-wielding hand from the corpse.

The bocor roared and struggled to rise as Steven applied Mrs. Flowers' staff and Mrs. Little hacked. The woman's eyes bulged and a glistening string of saliva drooled from her open mouth as she worked. Bones cracked beneath Steven's blows. Bits of clothing and flesh and splashes of still-hot blood flew with the frantic strokes of the ax.

Gator had backed off, letting Mrs. Little and his master deal with the upper body while she crushed the fingers of a hand that, though severed, was still crawling, nails scraping against the pine porch boards, as it tried to reach the .38.

The ax bit into the corpse's throat. Another chop and the head flew off the porch into the yard. Still the corpse struggled. Handless and headless, its chest and shoulders like so many pounds of chopped meat, it fought to rise.

"Stand back!" Mrs. Little yelled. She was blood-splashed

and disheveled, her face a homicidal mask. Steven backed away, almost as afraid of her as of the headless corpse. Mrs. Little gritted her teeth as she swung at the deputy's kneecaps. Steven grimaced at the grisly crunch of splintering bone.

Then Mrs. Little was backing away. The corpse—what was left of it—lay still. Steven staggered to the edge of the porch and upchucked the peas, mashed potatoes, and pork chop he'd had for supper. Gator stood at his heel and looked on sympathetically, her muzzle dripping scarlet.

A hand patted his shoulder when he finished heaving. "You okay?"

Steven nodded. He wasn't okay, probably never would be again after this, but he was alive and he knew he had to keep alert if he wished to remain so.

Avoiding the deputy's hacked body, his gaze sought the cabin's open door, lingered upon the still form lying inside. A scarlet pool glistened about the hoodoo woman's head. A pie-sized splotch soaked the front of her dress. The old woman's eyes were open, her expression one of surprise.

FROM THE TREE LINE, THE BOCOR, BACK IN LAMAR'S ruined body, watched the woman, the boy, and the dog go by. He had rid himself of the useless intestines, and the stomach flesh sagged like old canvas. The throat wound yawned like a second mouth. The corpse's nose and lips were in tatters, and one grey, cheesy-looking ear hung forward as if straining to hear what the departing figures had to say.

His anger—boundless, rapacious, and homicidal—was a blood frenzy, his imagination a red-frothing, rancid tantrum of hate. He envisioned a thousand deaths for the woman and the boy, all of them violent and excruciating, as he watched them vanish into the blackness between the trees.

TWENTY-ONE

Morning dawned and Steven was so glad to see the light at his window he quietly sobbed himself back to sleep.

A couple hours later, his mother called him to breakfast and, while he picked at his cereal, Mikey wanted to know where he had been last night. Steven hated to lie to his little brother, but no way was he going to answer that one—especially not in front of his mother.

"You tell me," he said to get Mikey off the subject. "Depends on what you were dreaming about."

Mikey responded by describing a nightmare in which the two of them had fled from a bleeding skeleton. Vividly picturing a fluorescent white skeleton glowing red and white against a background of dark forest, Steven shivered.

After breakfast, he wanted to go out. There was so much to do before the sun went down and Bloody Bones came for him. But he had to feed Gator and then his mother made him fetch his dirty laundry, which entailed a hunt under his bed and in his closet. When he finished, he left without asking Mom, who might have more chores for him. With Gator trotting by his side, he went to find Whitey.

The Creedy residence was as run down and as grey as the worst sharecropper shanty and not much bigger. Mr. Creedy's ancient Dodge flaked rust onto the oil-soaked drive, two of its tires were flat, and through the dust-coated, green-tinted windshield, he could see the torn and threadbare upholstery.

Steven had never been inside the house, nor did he have any desire to. He imagined it dirty and smelly, hopefully, for Whitey's sake, not as bad as Mr. Creedy's Dodge. Big iridescent bottle flies buzzed two uncovered garbage cans that stood beside the porch. Hearing raised voices as he neared, he halted in the dirt yard in front of the porch that was missing two of its grey, moss-grown boards and listened to Mr. and Mrs. Creedy insult each other. They sounded close to blows.

He was dreading the thought of knocking on the rickety screen door, when Whitey, who must have been looking out a window, came out, saying, "Come on, let's get away from here."

The younger boy's hands were shaking and his eyes looked haunted. His hair, which normally stuck up like an unevenly growing field of albino wheat, was plastered to his forehead; his stained tee shirt was far from white; his raggedy jeans, cut off above the knees, the frayed edges a fringe of white threads, were stiff with dried sweat. He needed a bath: Steven could smell him. And it wasn't his parents' arguing that had turned the flesh under his eyes grey; Whitey had seen Jimmy stabbed, had seen his throat cut open, his best friend brutally murdered. Steven felt a sharp pang for Whitey's grief and more than a little jealous of Jimmy for inspiring such devotion. Steven had friends, but he realized he was so average he'd probably never be anybody's best friend.

As they walked south along the shoulder of Peabody Road with the sun beating down on their heads and the smell of manure baking in the fields on either side of the dirt road filling their noses, Steven pulled a stick of Juicy Fruit chewing gum from his pocket, ripped it in half, paper and all, and offered a piece to Whitey.

"Thanks," Whitey accepted.

They spent a moment unwrapping the gum and getting it softened up; then Steven told Whitey about his encounter with the bocor the night before and how he'd seen Mrs. Flowers killed.

"She dead?" Whitey asked, wide-eyed when Steven had finished.

"Yep." Steven kicked a stone off the shoulder of the road into the drainage ditch, shuddered as he remembered just how dead she had looked with the chunk of scalp missing at her hairline.

"And you couldn't go to the police?"

"Nope. The police would be asking me questions all day, and I'm really scared of the sun going down before we find Lamar: because if we don't find him, he's going to find us."

Whitey shuddered. "I don't want to find Lamar," he said, watching a buzzard wheel in the hazy blue sky over the woods beyond the field.

"We have to."

"How?"

"Billy Bob's going to lead us to him."

Whitey's pale eyebrows shot up. "How's he going to do that? He's in the hospital clear over to Caledonia."

"Then we'll have to get him out, won't we?" Steven said and kicked another stone into the drainage ditch.

BILLY BOB WAS LOST.

And scared.

So scared the sweat trickling down his spine felt like ice water despite the throbbing heat of the swamp.

Slogging through the brackish, calf-deep water, poking the sandy bottom with a stick and keeping an eye out for snakes, it was easy to imagine he was in a jungle half a world away. Here and there, the late afternoon sunlight arrowing down through the cypresses and Spanish moss pierced the gloom and lay dazzling on the water. Soon, the sun would set, and the thought of getting caught here at night with quicksand awaiting his every step only increased his terror.

He had to be crazy to come out here like a criminal returning to the scene of the crime. He certainly felt like a criminal. A guilty one. Guilt was eating him up. He could feel it in his gut; it had grown teeth and was very hungry.

He swatted at the gnats and mosquitos that were constantly with him and which seemed at least as hungry as his guilt. Now the light was purpling, the gloom thickening under the forest canopy. If he followed the sunset light, he'd go west and come out, eventually, on Peabody, but once the sun set, he'd be wandering in circles. The thought spurred him along.

Now the last of the light was fading, and in the gathering twilight the moss-hung trees became giant tentacled creatures waiting to snatch him if he ventured too near. And as the colors drained into night, brown bark, green moss, white sand —all faded to an oppressive and cadaverous grey.

Billy Bob hurried, frantic now, splashing loudly, terror propelling his bare feet through the shallow water. Suddenly he stopped and backpedaled. His hands flung up defensively at the sight ahead.

In the last glow of dusk, leafless as it was and standing as it did in the center of the stream on its dark island, the dead cypress glowered against the sky. The lightning scar blazed down its flank was white as moonlight. He licked his lips. Now what? Say he was sorry? He hadn't brought a rope and wouldn't know how to haul the boy out anyway. This had been a stupid idea. He backed away, started to turn, to run—

And stopped...

Lamar stood before him, covered in quicksand; and when his grin broadened into a smile—split, peeling lips exposing blood-dripping teeth—quicksand spurted from his mouth, dribbled from his chin.

Billy Bob backed away. Lamar followed. Billy realized what the corpse was doing; Lamar was backing him toward the quicksand. Frantically, he poked the stick behind him. The stick went through the creek bottom. He was on the brink.

Lamar was reaching, eyes glowing in the gloom like small moons, blood glistening in the ruin of his throat. Billy swung the stick at the dead boy's head, but Lamar caught it and yanked it out of his hand.

While he was off balance, Lamar pushed him.

Billy scrambled wildly, arms pinwheeling. One foot went under, and he toppled full length with an epic splash. He was up to his waist instantly. Throwing himself forward, he dug into the sand trying to find solid ground. When the water reached his chin, he beat it furiously in a hideous parody of a dog paddle.

He wasn't sinking fast enough for Lamar, who pressed the stick into his collar bone, giving him an assist.

The quicksand touched his chin and he was staring up through the water at the leering corpse. Billy's cheeks bulged with his last breath, his lungs bursting with the need to scream.

He felt the stick on his forehead, pushing him backwards and down.

But now it was Pa's face grinning down at him as the quicksand poured into his throat, stifling his scream.

BILLY BOB'S EYES FLUTTERED OPEN. A HAND WAS clapped over his mouth.

"Shhh. It's me, Steven."

Billy Bob moaned through Steven's fingers. "Geez, Blankenship!" he said, peeling the hand off his mouth. "Trying to give me a heart attack?"

"Sorry, you started to scream when I tried to wake you."

"How'd you get here?" Billy swung his legs off the bed, adjusted the hospital gown, which seemed to be missing its most important parts.

"Hitched a ride." Steven went into the small closet. He tossed Billy his clothes. "Get dressed."

Billy caught the overalls and tee shirt. "How'd you get in here?"

"Easy." Blankenship looked him in the eye—something Billy couldn't remember him doing before; and though his expression didn't lose its seriousness, its slightly mad intensity, one corner of his mouth hooked into a grin. "It's visiting hours."

Billy took stock of Blankenship as he hauled on his overalls. Despite the haggard look in his eyes, the copper-haired boy looked tougher, more in control, than the old Steven Blankenship. Punching Skeeter had done the kid some good.

Despite everything he been through, Billy managed a grin. "'Visiting hour'... You monkey snot."

"Yeah, well hurry up. Whitey and Gator're waiting outside."

"I hate to ask you," Billy Bob said, pulling on his tee shirt, "but where are we going?"

"That's up to you. We've got to find Lamar."

"Lamar's dead." Billy spoke too quickly, but Blankenship knew, didn't he? He had as much as admitted that he and his dad had hidden Lamar's body when he'd threatened the others.

"You know better than that," Blankenship said.

Billy recalled, as he sat on the edge of the hospital bed and tied his beat-up Buster Browns, the mad laughter of the night before, the snapping of bones...the insane slurping... He

wished he could tell himself that the dead don't walk, and
that it was a living person who had killed his pa, but Billy had
seen the corpse's face, the hole in its throat. Rising, he
nodded.

"Yeah, come on."

He led the way to the door.

IT WAS LATE AFTERNOON AND OVERCAST BY THE TIME
they found the dead cypress. When they'd started out from
the Caledonia Hospital parking lot, it had still been sunny,
though several white clouds had moved in to clutter the
morning's blue. But hitching a ride back hadn't been as easy
as going out. They'd walked a third of the way along the
shoulder of the road—a good four miles—before an ancient
pickup, riding low on its springs under two bales of hay,
wheezed to a stop beside them and an equally ancient black
man had hooked a thumb toward the truck bed.

All the while they were on the road, Steven worried the
nurses would find Billy Bob missing and the Caledonia police
would pick them up. Steven imagined himself spending the
night in the Caledonia jail. After what he'd seen last night, he
didn't doubt Lamar could slip through the bars into his cell. If
the bocor, Bloody Bones, whoever the killer was, turned into a
puff of smoke before his eyes or grew wings and flew, he
would not be surprised.

And Lord...he had thought as his kidneys took a beating in
the truck bed...*about those times when I wondered if, maybe,*

you and Old Nick might be stories—like Bloody Bones—made up to scare kids...it won't happen again. Just get us through this.

Leaving the road after they were dropped off, they'd cut through the woods to the swamp and soon were slogging through calf-deep water as they followed a sandy-bottomed creek. Gator plowed tirelessly through water up her chest, dogpaddling when it got too deep. Steven kept an eye out for snakes as he poked the sand ahead with a stick. Soon, he saw why they had to follow the creek: it would have taken forever to pick their way through the undergrowth and over the thick spiders' legs of cypress roots that sprouted everywhere.

When they'd entered the swamp, he'd heard crows and jays, but the deeper they penetrated that melancholy region of shadows and water, the quieter it grew. Trees pressed like walls on either side, obscured the sky overhead. Except for the noise of their passing, the infrequent splash of a fish, and the ceaseless drone of insects, the swamp was silent.

Steven was looking down, poking the sand, when Billy Bob nudged him and pointed with his own dripping stick.

"There."

Steven and Whitey saw it at once, dead ahead, towering up and up like a fairy-tale giant. The ancient cypress, rising from a hillock surrounded by water and with its white lightning scar running down the length of the trunk on this side, drew a moan of fear from Steven. The tree's ancient shawl of moss, dead as the cypress, wafted ghostlike on the slight breeze.

"Now what?" Whitey asked when Billy Bob had led them to one side of the hillock and poked his stick under to show them where the edge of the quicksand hole was.

Whitey was addressing him, Steven realized; and, for the

first time, it occurred to him that, even though Billy Bob had guided them to Lamar's grave, he himself was leading this expedition; Billy and Whitey were waiting for him to speak. The grey sky and the smell of approaching rain infected Steven with a sense of urgency that allowed him no time to ponder the turnabout.

"Ain't thought that far ahead yet," he said, feeling frustrated and anxious. "I guess I figured we'd think of something when we got here."

After only a couple hours' restless sleep and trekking to Caledonia and back, what he really felt like doing was find a dry grassy spot and close his eyes (of course, the mosquitos would eat him alive and Bloody Bones would carve whatever was left). He had no words of wisdom, no plan of action to offer.

Whitey screwed up his face and scratched his white, sweat-slick hair. "'We?'" He shook his head, looked at his surroundings with dull, lackluster eyes. "All I can think of is runnin'." Billy Bob's ice-blue eyes, whites veined with red, stared into Whitey's, then met Steven's. Despite the bigger boy's sallow complexion and flabby-looking flesh, Steven was surprised to see such drive for survival in the former bully's gaze. Billy's fierce intensity didn't dispel the awful suffocating dread that enwrapped him along with the dampness and heat.

"You can't run from Bloody Bones." Billy managed a weak smile. "Sooner or later, he's gonna getcha!"

Whitey wasn't amused. "He ain't Bloody Bones."

"No, he's not," Steven said. "He's worse and we've got to stop him."

Billy Bob poked the quicksand. "You can't kill what's already dead."

"No, but maybe we can stop him." Steven slapped his stick against his palm. "Maybe bust him up so he can't walk or hold a knife."

"Maybe chop him up into little pieces!" Whitey said. Steven was glad to see the snarl on the boy's face.

"You got a knife?" Billy said.

"No," said Whitey. "Maybe we could take his; there's three of us."

Billy Bob sneered. "Yeah? Well, my pa was one tough guy, and bein' tough didn't help him none. Not a lick."

"Look," Steven said anxiously, his nerves stinging like red ant bites at the thought of doing nothing until it was too late. "We gotta do something. It's gonna get dark in here even before the sun sets."

Scowling, Billy Bob looked around, as if searching for something. He grunted and, throwing down his stick, wrestled a fair-sized rock from the mud between the dead cypress's roots. The stone splashed loudly and quickly sank into the quicksand when Billy hurled it. "Let's bury the fucker," he said.

"'The fucker'," Whitey echoed. He spat into the water over the quicksand, then busied himself clawing another rock out of the bank.

Steven joined in the hunt for rocks, but not before staring a long moment at the quicksand hole, as if Lamar's head were already parting the sand, pushing up through the water, the bocor's undead eyes fastening on his.

The dead wood and stones they turned up nearby quickly depleted, forcing them to go farther up and down stream, growing tired as the hours wormed laboriously by. Steven had ordered Gator ashore. She was a good girl and had listened, but each time he went off for another branch or chunk of log, he was haunted by the vision of his coming back and finding her missing and the quicksand closing over her head.

Steven stubbed his toe on a rock maybe fifty yards upstream. Digging it up, he found the stone to be sizable and only the anxiety that kept him wide awake gave him the strength to lug the small boulder back to the quicksand hole. Billy Bob, huffing from whatever he had just dumped in, helped him carry the rock the last few yards and dump it. Gator, standing on the hillock under the dead cypress, impatiently stamped her forepaws.

"It's getting dark," Steven panted as he watched the sand and water settle where the rock had disappeared.

"It's going to rain," Billy Bob said, panting beside him. The boy's face and arms and tee shirt were streaked with mud, his overhauls were soaked to the crotch, his Buster Brown's probably as full of sand as Steven's Paul Parrot's.

Steven looked up and, sure enough, not all of the gloom was caused by the tree shadows; while he had bent his attention to his toil, threatening grey clouds had moved in.

"Think we've dumped enough crap in there?" Steven said.

Billy swiped his face with the back of his forearm. "Probably not. We could be here all night filling the hole."

"I hate to think we did all that work just to make it easier for him to climb out."

"Don't say that."

Abruptly, the sky grew darker and a wind sprang up. Lightning flashed and thunder rolled over them.

"Whew, that breeze feels good," Billy Bob said, closing his eyes and facing the rising breeze. Steven shivered at the sudden rush of cool air over his sweaty body.

Whitey appeared, running, dragging a long branch that he threw down when he saw them. "Let's get out of here!" he bawled. "I got a bad feeling!"

On the bank, Gator whined.

The rain was sudden and intense. A cold drop splashed Steven's cheek. Then it was pouring, plastering his shirt to his body and churning the water. Thunder cracked, closer this time. Lightning flashed.

"Come on! Look how dark it's gotten!" Whitey shouted above the noise of the pelting rain. He tugged Steven's arm.

Steven started, as if from a trance. "Right." But before he could move, he heard a splash.

Then Whitey was flailing his arms and kicking at something. "He's got me!" Whitey wailed. "Help!"

Whitey fell on his back full length in the water and Steven saw him jerked toward the quicksand hole as if something had hold of his ankle.

Barking ferociously, Gator charged down the hillock and grabbed Whitey's tee shirt in her teeth and pulled, but the cotton tore and Whitey, shrieking hysterically, jerked forward again. His leg disappeared beneath the quicksand.

"HELP MEEEEE!"

The scream broke Steven's paralysis and he started for Whitey, but Billy Bob reached him first and grabbed the smaller boy under the arms. For a moment, it looked as if Billy and whatever had Whitey by the ankles were playing tug-of-war; then Billy was hauling Whitey to his feet. But now Billy's eyes bulged and his arms pinwheeled as his feet were yanked from under him. He went down with a splash, soaking Steven.

For a heartbeat, Billy Bob—roaring, head and shoulders

still out of the water—dug furiously at the edge of the pit. Steven rushed to help, but Billy was yanked under, leaving Steven with an afterimage of the terror in Billy Bob's eyes as his face disappeared under the sand.

A geyser erupted, spouted high into the air. And amid the rain of water and quicksand, Lamar burst from the pit. He landed, crouched, his peeling fingers outstretched.

"Come on!" Whitey was pulling his arm.

Steven's heart slammed into his ribs. He felt rooted, immovable. As if struggling under water, he forced himself to back away. He remembered to breathe. Then a second form burst from the geyser and landed beside Lamar. Squinting through the downpour, Steven stared in disbelief.

Mauser!

The dog's dead eyes met his through the sheeted rain. Then Mauser lifted his head to howl, and Steven beheld the gruesome gash that stretched under his chin like a second mouth.

TWENTY-TWO

W hitey was a grey shape on his left moving through the veils of rain; Gator was a smaller form loping on his right. Steven strained to catch any sounds of pursuit behind them, but if Lamar and Mauser were there, pounding after them, the sound of his and Whitey's and Gator's crashing through the pine wood and the noise of his own hitching breath and the ceaseless roar of the rain covered it.

Through the torrent, they had found their way out of the swamp, Steven leading, following blind instinct rather than landmarks. By the time they left the creek and plunged into the trees, the premature darkness had become near-total, lit only by frequent lightning flashes.

They burst from the pines into a cornfield, and immediately—out in the open without the trees hulking all around—the night seemed brighter. The tender, waist-high cornstalks bowed beneath the rain crashed underfoot. The furrowed earth had turned to mud and was harder to run in than the creek bed.

Approaching the far side of the field, Steven looked over his shoulder, hoping to catch sight of Lamar if he was there, hoping even harder that he wasn't—and stumbled and fell when his foot jammed down into a shallow irrigation ditch. His hands sank in mud up to his wrists. Without rising, he twisted around, terrified that Mauser would be there to knock him flat on his back. Lightning flashed, turning the cornfield startlingly white for a moment, flashed again. Steven let out his breath, panted as he leaned on his hands, continuing to scan. Lamar and Mauser weren't in sight.

Whitey dropped beside him, heedless of the mud. The boy's narrow chest heaved with exertion. Gator stood alert, ears cocked, as he stared back the way they had come. Thunder cracked and boomed above the rain.

"Billy Bob saved me," Whitey whispered when he could speak. "Why'd he do that?"

Steven's brain was too numb to think of an answer. He raised a muddy hand palm-up in a half-hearted shrug.

"He died instead of me."

Whitey's expression, Steven saw the next time lightning flashed, was one of grief and confusion. Steven didn't understand it either; he would have thought Billy Bob was the type to throw somebody into the path of disaster to save himself. Billy Bob had changed. Perhaps the confrontation with death and the struggle to survive (*and the fear—don't forget the fear*) had changed them all. He certainly wasn't the same Steven Blankenship as the boy who ran and puked the day Lamar died and who was forever impatient with rainy days and

Mikey's endless barrage of how and why's. He thought if he could find a way to defeat the bocor, he would be happy to answer Mikey's questions for a month straight.

A long desperate sigh rattled out of Whitey, followed by a weary "Oh God!"

"What?" Steven leaned closer.

"I miss Jimmy!" Whitey sobbed.

Not knowing what else to do, Steven did as he had the first time Whitey cried in his presence: he placed his hand on his friend's shoulder. Skeeter, if he was still alive, would have called Whitey a crybaby, and, a week ago, Steven himself might have agreed; but a week ago his knowledge of why people cried had been limited to spankings and his goldfish dying when he was five because he had been too lazy to change the water.

A low warning growl issued from Gator's throat and Steven stood, impatient for lightning to flash again. When it did, he saw a narrow, rutted dirt road running alongside the irrigation ditch. In that second before the world plunged back into darkness, he thought he glimpsed movement. Then lightning flashed again, and he saw through the curtain of rain, Lamar and Mauser loping toward them.

"Run!" he screamed and shoved Whitey ahead of him. Fueled by terror and his pounding heart, he dug his heels into the muddy road. In the next lightning flash, he glimpsed a farmhouse up a long sloping yard. The lights were off, but maybe the owners were sleeping.

"The house!" he shouted and took off across the lawn.

Lightning flashed. Steven saw a battered pickup truck alongside the house and, down the slope, a stone well with a pitched roof and a hand crank to draw the bucket. The grass was slippery under Steven's shoes, but his terror-driven momentum propelled him on.

Ahead, to the right of the well and between Steven and the house, Mauser blocked their way. Steven slowed; his heart punched his ribs. Lamar appeared behind them. Washed free of quicksand, the wounds in his gut and his throat glistened; here and there white bones gleamed through the rotting flesh. Something long and metallic flashed in the corpse's hand.

"Look out, Whitey! He's got a knife!"

Seen intermittently in the lightning flashes, Lamar advanced. One ear was gone, reduced to pulpy strings that hung down and clung to his neck like melted mozzarella; the other was a grey flower alive with milk-white maggots. More maggots writhed like living snot in the noseless pit in the middle of his face. Decaying lips were peeled back in a savage grin. A wild, malicious light glowed in the creature's dead eyes.

In stark contrast, the Doberman stood like a statue, its gaze as lightless as a stuffed animal's glass eyes. The fangs bared between snarling lips might have been a product of a taxidermist's art.

Steven and Whitey backed toward the well. Gator stayed with them, fidgeting in circles as she growled menacingly now at Lamar, now at Mauser, now looking to her master for guidance. Thunder cracked, and Steven saw Lamar standing a couple of yards away.

"Gotcha, Blankenship!"

Steven heard the gritty whisper issue from the blackness and backed away. A glance over his shoulder showed him Mauser hadn't moved. The dog was a silhouette like a

Halloween cutout snipped from black construction paper. Rough wet stones stopped Steven's retreat. The rim of the well pressed against his back. Lamar's free hand shot out and Steven gasped as the corpse's tattered fingers clutched the front of his tee shirt. Steven raised his hands to ward off the knife that flashed in the lightning.

Gator caught Lamar's wrist in her wide jaws and gave it a savage wrench. The crunch of breaking bones was music to Steven's ears. The knife fell, and, for a second in the strobing light, it looked to Steven as if his dog and Lamar's corpse were dancing. Steven snatched the knife from the grass. It was a butcher knife like the one Deputy Riley's corpse had wielded. That the bocor had found another one wasn't surprising: every kitchen and smoke house in the county had at least one. The wooden handle was slimy with putrid flesh. The contact repelled Steven, but he gripped the weapon as if his life depended on it.

With a roar and a string of curses in a strange tongue, Lamar hurled Gator aside and leaped on Steven. Caught off guard, Steven smashed backwards against the well. The impact knocked the breath out of him. Lamar grabbed him by the throat. The hand was as cold and slimy as a frozen fish starting to thaw. Though the back of the wrist was laid open, exposing broken bones, the tendons were intact, and curling his fingers around Steven's Adam's apple in a deadly grip, Lamar bent him backwards over the black shaft. Lamar's good hand crept up his wrist, working its way toward the knife. The corpse reeked of swamp mud and rotting meat. Steven tasted bile. His vision swam. The rain blowing in under the wellhouse roof peppered his staring eyes.

Pale hands appeared from behind Lamar, dug into the

corpse's cheeks. Lamar's head thrashed as he tried to shake Whitey off. Decayed muscles tore. A long flap of flesh hung from Lamar's jaw, exposing teeth and grey receding gums. Steven yanked his hand free and slammed the knife into Lamar's shoulder. The blade grated against the corpse's collar bone. Lamar's hand closed on his wrist, forced the blade out. Afraid Lamar would turn the knife on him, Steven flipped it into the well.

Then Lamar was reeling behind him, battling at Gator, who had sprung onto his back and latched her teeth into his shoulder. Lamar went down under the pit bull's weight. Taking advantage, Gator shifted her hold to the open wound in Lamar's throat, her powerful teeth chomping through bone and cartilage and decomposing meat.

Lamar hurled his assailant off. Gator landed with a mouthful of flesh. Lamar's head hung at a peculiar angle as he rose, as if it were trying to rest on his shoulder.

A long roll of thunder passed over them, followed by a resounding *crrrrack!* In the flickering light, Steven saw that the glow had gone out of Lamar's eyes. The cadaver stood as statue-still as Mauser, its eyes as empty as the windows of a vacant store.

"Look!" Whitey shrieked.

Steven wheeled. Not three yards away, Mauser moved. Evil intelligence shone in the dog's psychotic eyes. Awe washed over Steven as he understood: the bocor could animate both bodies but inhabit only one at a time. The realization gave him courage in spite of the deadly fix he was in. That which was vulnerable could be defeated.

Snarling, Mauser leaped at Whitey. Gator silently intercepted, lunging for the wound in the bigger dog's throat.

Mauser ducked and Gator chomped into the muscle of the Doberman's jaw and began frenziedly thrashing her head like a rat terrier killing a rodent by drumming it on the ground. The big dog pawed at the pup, but Gator hung on, easing her bite only to get a firmer hold. Mauser's teeth, chomping ferociously, snapped on empty air. Gator jumped back, landed on her hind legs, forepaws in the air like a rearing stallion, and sprang forward again. Her jaws locked on one of Mauser's forelegs. A savage twist of her head and Steven heard a *snap* like a stick broken over a knee. Steven rejoiced in the sound. Mauser chomped. Gator ducked, jumped on Mauser's back, clamped her jaws on the big dog's spine and wrapped her legs around the Doberman in a bear hug. The dogs rolled. Gator locked onto the corpse. Mauser tried to shake her off. Steven and Whitey urged the pup on.

The Doberman went down. Gator jumped off, panting, legs braced. Mauser rose on three legs; the fourth dangled uselessly. The dog's great head, attached to the neck stump by broken vertebrae and a strip of black-haired meat, dragged on the wet grass. The glow faded from the monster's eyes, its jaws stopped champing, and its body collapsed.

The rain was slacking off, the breeze falling. The thunder, booming overhead a minute ago, was moving away. Lightning flashed in the distance.

A cheer died in Steven's throat as he realized, too late, that he and Whitey should have dumped Lamar's body into the well while the dogs were fighting. In the strobing light, the corpse moved—a flame flickered in the dead, lackluster eyes, flared like the wick of a kerosene lantern turned all the way up. Reanimated, Lamar seized Whitey and slammed him against the well. "*Unnn!*" The stones knocked the wind out of him. Teetering on the lip of the well, wild with fear, Whitey pounded his fists into Lamar's face. He knocked out a tooth but failed to dislodge the lopsided grin. Whitey gasped for air. His heels drummed against the wet stones.

Gator tore into the dead boy's leg. Steven grabbed Lamar in a headlock. Wrapping one arm around the cadaver's neck and grasping his wrist, he tried to wrench the head from the body. Though Gator had half completed the job, the task was beyond Steven. Gator spat out a chunk of calf and tore into the other leg.

Lamar bashed Steven in the temple. Steven staggered back, seeing stars. Half blinded from the blow, Steven swung his fist in a wild haymaker and connected solidly with Lamar's precariously leaning head. A loud *crack!* and Lamar's head was tilting back, looking off into the night over his shoulder. Roaring, the bocor released Whitey and turned. Steven raised an arm to ward off the blow. Gator pounced, barreling into Lamar's chest, locking her jaws on what was left of the corpse's throat.

Lamar—top heavy with Gator clinging to him—slammed against the well, teetered, and went over backwards, headfirst down the shaft, kicking the bucket loose as he fell.

"*Nooo!*" Steven rushed forward in time to hear the splash. Whitey, who had thrown himself off the well, rose shakily from the grass.

"Gator!" Steven yelled down the black shaft and was rewarded with a series of barks echoing hollowly from below. Steven released the oak bucket and spun the crank handle letting the bucket hurl to the water below. "Come on Gator! Up, Girl!" The rope jerked taut and the bucket gained weight.

Too much weight for the burden to be just the thirty-pound dog.

"Help!" Steven shouted. Whitey grabbed the handle from the other side, and together they hauled. Snarls and barks echoed up the shaft. Steven imagined the pup snapping at the hands clinging to the bucket. The rope bucked crazily, and it was all Steven and Whitey could do to keep the crank from leaping from their hands. A splash followed a sudden lightening of the bucket.

The rain had stopped during the fight. The thunder and lightning were moving away. The moon broke through the clouds. In another moment Steven rejoiced to see the big pup hanging out of the bucket, one paw wrapped around the rope.

"Good girl!" he cried as he and Whitey secured the bucket. Gator insisted on helping by leaping out and they both ended up on the ground. Gator was first to rise and stood over her master shaking water from her fur.

"Listen," Whitey said, staring into the darkness of the well.

Steven joined him. Tentacles of fear crept up his spine as he realized it wasn't over yet. Sounds, like fingers scratching at stone, came from below. And little splashes like loose mortar falling. Then a big splash—as if Lamar had hauled himself part way out of the water and fallen back in.

"Oh, Jesus!" Whitey said. "He's not giving up, is he?"

Mauser was rising. The moon had escaped the clouds, and by its light, Steven watched the Doberman lurch toward them on its three unbroken legs. Its head lolled on its shoulder. Malevolent eyes glared at them from a grotesque angle.

Gator was on the big dog in a flash, tearing at the strip of meat that connected its head to its torso. In seconds, the head, still chomping, an all-too-human hatred burning in its blood-shot eyes, rolled away. The Doberman's body didn't topple but dragged itself after its head. Gator attacked the other foreleg. Mauser toppled, but Gator held on, thrashing her head and digging her paws into the wet grass. The one leg cracked. Gator backed away. Incredibly, the crippled torso was again struggling to rise.

Steven glanced at Whitey. The younger boy was on his knees, retching.

"Come on!" Steven yelled, his own stomach heaving. "We gotta dump Mauser in the well!"

Whitey rose shakily, wiped his mouth. "Leave it. It can't hurt us. Let's get out of here." Whitey's eyes were big and round and staring and he seemed jumpy as a cat.

Steven shook his head. "Un uh. Look!" He pointed at Mauser's head.

Lying on its side, the head glared at them, nose wrinkled, lips drawn back exposing its teeth in a silent snarl.

Suddenly, the head flew over the grass like a bowling ball, bounded as if its rush had encountered a bump, and latched its teeth onto Whitey's leg.

"*Aiiii!*" In the moonlight, Whitey performed a grotesque one-legged dance.

"Get it, Gator!" Steven yelled, and Gator attacked, snapping at the head, biting it on the mouth and snout. The head dropped to the ground, pivoted and snapped at Gator. Teeth bared, Gator jumped high, twisted in the air and pounced, clamping her teeth into Mauser's jaw, beating the head noisily into the soggy earth.

Steven, his body shaking violently, flesh crawling, grabbed the head by the ears and pitched it into the well.

The torso was moving, hobbling on the broken stumps of its ruined forelegs; dark fluids oozed from its neck stump. Steven seized a hind leg. Whitey limped over and took hold of the other. Together, they hauled the torso to the well, hefted it atop the low stone rim—each averting his gaze from the raw horror of the neck—and shoved it in. The splash was tremendous.

"We did it! We did it!" Whitey shouted. His voice trembled with emotion. "We killed Bloody Bones!"

"No, we didn't," Steven said, resisting the impulse to celebrate. He looked up at the full moon riding in and out of the clouds and an image came to his mind: Billy Bob poking the quicksand with his stick. "You can't kill what's already dead," he told Whitey.

Whitey's eyes grew big with fresh fear, and he looked at the well as if expecting Lamar's hand to appear on the rim. It didn't, but the scratching noises below had started again.

"Oh Lord!" Whitey moaned. "He's trying to get out!"

Unless the body is destroyed or imprisoned, Steven remembered Mrs. Flowers saying. He scanned the moonlit yard for anything he could hurl down the well, but saw nothing useful.

The scratching noises seemed nearer now. Peering down the shaft, he saw only blackness beyond the few feet of stones bathed in the moonlight.

I Bloody Bones, an' I comin' to get you.

The voice snagged ice-cold fishhooks into Steven's brain. He shuddered as if gelatinous slugs were worming a slime trail down his spine. He clenched his teeth and shoved at the stones, but none plummeted into the hole. The mortar between the grey blocks was crumbling, soft enough to dig out with a crowbar if he had the time, which he didn't.

I goin' to cut your heart out, Blankenship. Can't you feel my cold hand on your heart, Boy?

And Steven did feel the dead hand upon his heart, freezing talons pressing into the soft pulsing meat, almost to the point of puncturing. He clutched his chest like an old man on the verge of a stroke.

Can't you feel me squeezing?

Any second now, the fingers would burst through the organ's delicate walls, spilling his life's blood, affording him one last shock before he plummeted into Death's gaping maw.

Steven's head snapped back. His eyes ping-ponged in their sockets, then focused on Whitey...

His cheek stung. Whitey had slapped him. "Wake up, Steven!" Whitey yelled in his face. "He's in your head! You almost fell in! He wants your body!"

And so he had. Even now with Whitey pulling on him, he was leaning precariously over the abyss, dizzy, a bloating nausea rising in his gullet at the thought that he had nearly joined the bocor at the bottom of the well.

I Bloody Bones, an' I comin' to get you.

Raucous laughter echoed through Steven's skull. The scratching sounds began again. Frantically, Steven looked around for anything he could use to pry the stones loose.

His gaze slid over it at first, then went back in a doubletake.

The pickup truck.

"Come on!" he yelled and took off up the gently rising lawn. Whitey limped after him.

Dented and rust-red all over, its front bumper hanging

crooked, the pickup also had a flat. Steven wondered if it would mire in the wet ground as he tried the door handle. The door opened with a loud screech.

Steven glanced at the farmhouse. No light came on, and no face emerged from behind the moonlit curtains. The noise of the storm had hidden the battle.

"You ain't got the key!" Whitey wailed.

"Don't matter. I don't know how to drive. I figure we could just roll it into the well."

Steven examined the foot pedals. The little pedal all the way to the left was the clutch. Though his dad's Oldsmobile was an automatic, his Uncle Pete's had a shifter, and he'd watched him let off the clutch while pressing down the gas pedal.

That won't work! The truck's not running! Like a mouse scratching in the pantry, panic gnawed at his thoughts. *Concentrate!*

Neutral. His father's shifter, mounted on the steering column, had an "N" which Dad explained allowed the car to roll without starting up.

He looked for the emergency brake, found it. It was rusted in place; he'd have to hope it was off. He tried the shifter; it didn't budge. Then he remembered to depress the clutch and thunked the shifter into neutral. He jumped out, checked that the front wheels were pretty much aimed toward the well, and hollered, "Okay, let's push!"

With his right hand on the steering wheel, Steven put his shoulder against the open door and leaned into it, digging his feet into the soggy ground.

"Push!" he yelled when the truck went nowhere.

"I am pushing!" Whitey yelled back through gritted teeth. Gator barked at the truck.

Steven's heart pounded. He pictured Lamar's corpse digging its fingers into the mortar, working its way up stone by stone, and finally emerging, hauling itself over the rim. The truck started to roll.

"Keep pushing!"

Whitey grunted something incomprehensible.

Despite the flat tire, the truck picked up speed. Steven jumped onto the running board and hauled himself in. Bouncing onto the driver's seat, he saw the truck had veered to the left when he'd grabbed the steering wheel to pull himself in. He wrenched the wheel to the right, oversteered, wrenched left.

He intended to jump at the last moment, but the well and the incredibly jolting, truck-stopping impact came up fast.

SOMEONE WAS SLAPPING HIM. ONE SIDE OF HIS FACE was wet and he decided he was bleeding. Remembering the truck, he opened his eyes. Whitey stood on the running board, leaning in. Gator was in the passenger seat, licking his ear.

"Geez, I thought you were dead!" Whitey clapped his hand over his heart to show his relief.

Steven sat up straight. "Is—?" He didn't have to finish the question or peer through the cracked windshield to view the demolished well house: in Whitey's broad smile, he saw their success.

When the farmer, hearing the crash and waking beside his half-deaf wife, hauled himself out of bed and looked out the window, he saw his truck wrecked and the well house caved in. The peaked roof lay on the hood of the pickup. Beside the truck, he saw two boys and a dog, dancing like pagans beneath the full moon.

The End

ACKNOWLEDGMENTS

IN APPRECIATION

My Granny, born Lima Francis McFarland in Shelby, North Carolina, in 1897, married twice, first to Lloyd Howell, with whom she had five children, the younest of which was my mother Virginia Ruth, then to a person she referred to as "Old Man Hendricks." Both men were alcoholics and died before I was born. Lima grew up, as most southerners did back then, not rich. She went to work in the Bibb City Cotton Mill in Columbus, Georgia, when she was twelve. She survived Scarlet Fever. (She told me her hair fell out but grew back.)

Granny was a red head, though her hair was grey by the time I came along, and snow-white by the time I was a pre-teen. Her hair was long and fell to her waist. She wore it in a bun by day but let it out before going to bed. I remember brushing it a few times as a boy. She was also the main cook in our home. I can almost smell her cornbread hot from the oven. She let me mix batter and icing, and I always got a chocolate cake on my birthday.

She never learned to read or write, but she would sound out lines in the Bible, tracing the words with a forefinger in the big family tome spread in her lap. But the woman was a storyteller. Some of my favorite memories of childhood are of my Granny telling me bedtime stories about Bloody Bones or the headless man searching for his head on the train tracks. These would generally end up with an "I gotcha!" and attendant tickling.

Her Bloody Bones stories were of two varieties. There were the ones where BB is on the porch. "Can't you hear the chair rocking? Bloody Bones is coming to get you. He's in the living room. Can't you hear the floor creak? BB is coming to get you. BB is on the stair. Listen. Did you hear that step squeak? The one your daddy's been meaning to fix?" And so on until he was in the room and you were hiding your head under the sheet, enthralled and more tense with the knowing the tickling was coming than from fear.

The other version involved a youngster playing in the yard with one of his mother's kitchen knives, flipping it into the dirt between his feet. He gets called to dinner, but his mother asks him where's her knife. He says he forgot it in the yard and goes to get it, but it's gone. She tells him to go to the neighbors' houses and don't come back without it. So he goes down the lane, house by house, knocking on the door and asking, "Have you seen my mother's knife?" The answer is no. Each house is a different color. He stops at the blue one, the red one, the yellow one. It's dark now. The road is a dead end. Beyond is the cemetery. The last house before the graveyard is painted black. He's terrified as he steps onto the porch and hesitates to knock on the door. But his mother told him not to come home without her knife. He knocks. The door opens. It's so dark inside he can barely see the man standing in the doorway. He imagines he's looking at a skeleton, its clothes and bones all bloody. But it's just his imagination. He's scared, that's all. His mind is playing tricks on him. Still, his voice trembles as he asks, "Have you seen my mother's knife?"

"Yes," says a voice from the shadows. And Bloody Bones steps forward, his skeletal hand clutching the missing knife. "And here it is!"

And Granny would make believe she was stabbing me in the chest. I would be expecting it, but I would cringe anyway. But before the imaginary blade pierced my heart, the tickling began.

Besides being a born storyteller and a fantastic cook, Granny knew a thing or two about hoodoo. She told me how when her oldest boy, my Uncle Obie, had a fever, she caught a bull frog and tied it to his foot to draw the fever out. The next day the frog was dead, and Obie's fever was gone.

Thank you, Granny.

Made in the USA
Middletown, DE
15 August 2025

11543592R00123